THE PIRATE RAID

Hero wasted neither time nor opportunity but leapt at the closest pirate and sliced his cowl-hidden head clean from his body. Down went the man without a sound—without even a crimson spurt of blood—and another sprang to take his place. This one Hero stabbed in the heart, his sword passing through the fellow as if he were made of cheese ... except that when Hero dragged the blade free the man failed to fall but kept right on fighting!

Out of instinct and desperation Hero struck again, and this time his blade tore aside the pirate's hood. Beneath it—

—A fleshless skull leered with empty sockets and rotting teeth!

He was fighting a corpse, a dead man who felt nothing and continued the battle secure in the knowledge that he could not die twice!

D0834857

Look for these Tor books by Brian Lumley

BRIAN LUMLEY

SHIP OF DREAMS

A TOM DOHERTY ASSOCIATES BOOK
NEW YORK

This is a work of fiction. All the characters and events portrayed in this book are fictitious, and any resemblance to real people or events is purely coincidental.

SHIP OF DREAMS

Copyright ©1986 by Brian Lumley

All rights reserved, including the right to reproduce this book, or portions thereof, in any form.

Cover art by Tim Jacobs

A Tor Book
Published by Tom Doherty Associates, Inc.
175 Fifth Avenue
New York, N.Y. 10010

Tor® is a registered trademark of Tom Doherty Associates, Inc.

ISBN: 0-812-52420-9

First Tor mass market printing: January 1994

Printed in the United States of America

0 9 8 7 6 5 4 3 2 1

CONTENTS

Down and Out in Celephais

Leewas Nith, High Magistrate of Celephais, leaned forward across the massive, raised oaken bench in the city's main courtroom and frowned down his long thin nose at the two men brought before him. While they were dressed in clothes of dream's styling—clothes which were a little stained and travel-worn, but still rather fine clothes for a pair of rogues such as these—it was plain to any practiced eye that they were not normal citizens of dream. No, these were or had been men of the waking world, who through the circumstance of death on their home plane now abided on this one.

Their sort was not especially rare in dreams; occasionally they occupied places of great prominence and power; though more often than not they merely merged into the background of the dreamlands, settled down and became one with the land of Earth's dreams. Not this pair, however, whose names were bywords in civilized places for brawling, thievery, drunkenness and illicit wenching.

They were Eldin the Wanderer and David Hero (or Hero of Dreams, as the latter seemed to be known, though why his sort of ruffian should be accorded so lordly a dream-name was anybody's guess) and the charges leveled against them on this occasion were typical of their record. Not so much heinous as outrageous; more mischievous than menacing.

Namely, they were accused of assault, seduction and arson, though not in that order. Oh, yes, and also drunkenness, non-payment of debts and vagrancy. Aye, and one or two other things to boot. Fortunately for them, Leewas Nith was a judge in more senses than the merely judiciary. He instinctively knew the characters of people. Even men from the waking world . . .

Not that he was blind to the faults of this pair, on the contrary, and he was sure that they were indeed guilty of many of the charges brought against them. But not all of them. Drunkenness, certainly. Indeed the older man, Eldin the Wanderer, must still be a little drunk if the tale he was just this minute done with telling was anything to go by. So utterly marvelous an invention had it been—of black wizardry and derring-do, of mountain-scaling and keep-climbing, of fierce battles with all manner of demon gods, plants and beings—that the courtroom had been held spellbound. Now the tale was told and its teller stood silent beside his younger companion. Now, too, Leewas Nith peered down the length of this thin nose, regarded the pair, considered his judgment.

Eldin the Wanderer and David Hero—Hah! And the High Magistrate silently snorted his displeasure as he recalled many talks of roguery heard in connection with these two. Well, they would rogue no more in Celephais, not when he was done with them. And Celephais would not be the first of dreamland's cities and towns to expel them. Not by a long shot. As for their tale—of how they came to arrive in Celephais in the first place and their "reasons" for doing the thoroughly unreasonable things they had done here—well, this Eldin fellow was obviously just as much a storyteller as a wanderer! Possibly more so. And Leewas Nith silently snorted to himself a second time.

"Eldin," he finally said, his voice brittle but at the same time full of a dire judicial strength. "You, Wanderer, as you are called. You tell an amusing, indeed a marvelous tale. Why, if the court is to believe you, then we now stand in the presence of two of the greatest heroes dreamland has ever known!"

"Oh, I wouldn't go so far," growled the bearded, burly, oddly-gangling man called Eldin, "but that's near enough." He twisted his scarred face into a scowl, rattled his chains and held them up. "And richly rewarded for our efforts, too!"

The High Magistrate continued as were he never interrupted. "And then misfortune befell you. On the day of your wedding-to-be, in Ilek-Vad your future wife woke up from the dreamlands and returned to the waking—" But here Eldin gave such a groan, and slumped against a pillar in so abject an attitude, that his younger friend was obliged to take hold of him and maintain him in an upright position.

"Did you have to remind him?" shouted David Hero, patting his apish companion's huge, pain-racked shoulder with a chained hand. "Damn me, that's the reason he gets drunk in the first place—because he can't forget Aminza Anz! What would you do if your bride-to-be woke up and left you stranded here in dreamland?"

While the rest of the court gasped at Hero's audacity, and while Hero himself glared all about at them where they sat, the High Magistrate merely frowned his annoyance. "Young man," his voice finally crackled, "I will not suffer such outbursts in my own courtroom. You and your companion were brought before me to answer certain charges, not to tell fantastic stories and perform stirring dramas and tragedies." He held up a sheet of parchment. "These are the charges you must answer:

"One: that you, David Hero, seduced Arkim Sallai's daughter, Misha, betrothed of Garess Nard. How do you answer the charge?"

Hero could not quite stifle a grin, his white teeth flashing from between lips which refused to be pursed. "Seduced?" he chuckled. "You mean when she invited me to stay the night in her garret room over her old man's tavern?"

"Guilty!" snapped Leewas Nith, this time with an audible snort. "Two: that when Arkim Sallai and Garess Nard heard the girl's cries of distress and came to her rescue—"

"*Her* cries of distress?" Hero was astounded. "Hers? They were my cries, not hers! Why, man, I'll carry scars down my back for the rest of my dream-life. That girl has nails as long as—"

"—Then that you knocked both of them down and broke Garess Nard's jaw!" finished the magistrate, his voice rising even as he rose sternly to his feet.

Hero gritted his teeth and slitted his eyes. "That Garess Nard," he growled. "The cowardly dog! Coming at a man with a hatchet like that. And me naked and weaponless and all . . . Well, almost?"

"Guilty!" cried Leewas Nith, leaning forward with his knuckles on the bench. "And if you make one more outburst I'll have both of you thrown into a dungeon for a year!"

He turned his gaze upon Eldin the Wanderer and slowly sat down again. Eldin, sensing the magistrate's eyes upon him, gave one last sob and looked up through red-rimmed, bloodshot eyes. "And you," said Leewas

Nith, "you boozy barrel of a man. What of the charges against you?"

"Charges?" grunted Eldin disinterestedly, his almost volcanic rumble full of misery. "What charges? Damn it to hell, I'm a hero, I tell you! We both are. And anyway, I don't remember a damned thing."

"Nor would you," answered Leewas Nith sharply, "if the charges are correct! Now hear them out in silence:

"One: that you, Eldin the Wanderer, having put up at the tavern of Arkim Sallai—(a), drank for a week of the best wines and then refused to pay the bill. And (b), when the master of the house refused you more drink, broke into the cellar, barricaded yourself in and continued to drink. And (c), when finally you fell into a drunken stupor and were thrown forcibly out into the street, then that you set fire to the place, much to the distress of its proprietor and patrons who were obliged to flee while the tavern burned to the ground!

"There were many witnesses to these crimes and they are not to be denied . . . Both you and Hero were later apprehended trying to leave town on a little-used caravan route disguised as priests of the Elder Gods, which is surely a rank outrage and a blasphemy in itself! Now what have you to say to all of this?"

Eldin wiped his eyes with his sleeve and glanced at Hero. He sniffled a little but then, as he noticed the corners of Hero's mouth twitching into a barely suppressed grin, jutted his chin and frowned a black frown. Hero's grin broadened until it became contagious. The two almost began to chuckle—before Hero managed to turn his choked laughter into a cough which he hid with the back of his hand. Eldin somehow followed suit, but only with great difficulty.

Finally the Wanderer turned his red eyes back up to the High Magistrate where he sat in judgment. "Can't a man have a little fun in dreamland anymore?" he asked. "Home from the wars, as it were, and never a flag waved and no welcome mat to greet us? Why, if Celephais weren't such a dead and alive den of dodderers you'd all have heard of us by now. Heroes, we are, and—"

"And we *have* heard of you," Leewas Nith cut him short. "We've heard far too much of you! Now be still while I pass judgment."

"Judgment nothing!" cried Hero. "I want to see Kuranes."

Again a gasp of astonishment went up from the courtroom, and Hero glared at the richly robed spectators and city councilors and junior judges where they sat upon their tiers of oaken benches. He felt like some sort of gladiator in an arena, except that there was nothing here to fight. And what with these chains, well, fighting was impossible anyway.

"Kuranes?" said Leewas Nith, as if he were hearing things. "King Kuranes? He does not try common criminals."

"Not so much of the 'common,' magistrate, if you don't mind," Hero bridled.

"And be careful who you call criminals," growled Eldin. "Are you deaf, man? We're *heroes*! Kuranes could verify it easily enough. So could you, for that matter. A carrier pigeon to Ilek-Vad across the Twilight Sea . . . you'd know the facts of things by this time tomorrow. I tell you that less than a month ago I dined with Randolph Carter himself, in Ilek-Vad. They're great friends, Carter and Kuranes, and I'm sure the king of Celephais wouldn't see a couple of heroes such as we are falsely accused."

Leewas Nith could control himself no longer. His wisdom remained—his natural kindness and understanding of the human condition, too—but his patience had been stretched to its very limits. "You are *not* falsely accused!" he snapped. "And even if you were heroes, we couldn't allow you to run rampant through the cities of dreamland. You must be punished."

"Punished?" cried the two together.

"Be quiet!" roared Leewas Nith, and he gave a signal to four heavily muscled Pargan orderlies where they stood to the rear of the chained men. The black, golden-kilted orderlies moved closer to the pair, tripped them, forced them to their knees and held them there.

"Be thankful Kuranes is not here," the High Magistrate told them. "Especially you, Eldin the Wanderer. King Kuranes loves his Celephais and would doubtless punish you fearfully for burning a piece of it down. Fortunately the tavern of Arkim Sallai was full of beetle and due for demolition, else I, too, would punish you most severely.

"And you, David Hero," and he turned his gaze upon the younger man. "Or Hero of Dreams, as you are styled. You too may be thankful, for the Garess Nard has agreed to wed Misha Sallai despite the ruin which your rapaciousness must otherwise visit upon her reputation. And so I shall be lenient with you also. But now I tire of all this and must therefore bring it to a close." He glared down upon them where they were obliged to kneel.

"When you were caught leaving the city you were carrying a great deal of money in your purses. This despite your many debts. Well, the money was confiscated and will be used in part to cover Arkim Sallai's unpaid bills. Moreover, there is sufficient to build him a new tavern; and so your crimes will have caused only a minimum of suffering. As for your yaks, your swords and fine clothes: they shall be auctioned off to pay compensation to Garess Nard for his broken jaw. Finally, Celephais is forbidden to you for a full year. You will be escorted to that same spot where you were apprehended and there set free—on foot! If you dare to return within a twelvemonth—" he shrugged. "Then it's the dungeons for both of you. That is all. I have spoken."

"What?" howled Hero and Eldin in concert.

"Take them away," said Leewas Nith to the Pargan orderlies. "Let my instructions be carried out to the letter."

"And are we to be sent into exile naked as babes?" cried Hero.

"Eh?" murmured the High Magistrate, already heading toward an arched doorway in the wall of the courtroom behind his judge's bench. He turned back for a moment to gaze at the two where they were being dragged away down an aisle under the steeply climbing tiers of seats. "No, no, not naked," he answered. "You will be given some clothes of good leather. Not so rich as the ones you wear now, no, but more in keeping with your . . . history?" Finally he smiled a thin smile and wagged a finger at the pair. "A lesson to both of you— and be glad I am merciful!"

Lions as Lambs

Eldin thumped the hard ground with an even harder fist and spat his frustration into the sand. "Merciful, the old windbag called himself," he said, digging Hero in the ribs. "Merciful, eh?"

"Can't you make a point without sticking your great fat elbow in me?" Hero grumbled, rubbing his side. "Look, I'm just as unhappy as you are, but all said and done I reckon we got off light. I mean, we could be rotting in some dungeon right now."

They lay side by side on their stomachs in a clump of long, spiky yellow grass, gazing through its fringes upon the distant spires of Celephais. The city was sprinkled with the lights of a thousand lanthorns now that night was descending; and long shadows, cast by the early crescent moon which stood almost clear of the hills to the north of the city, lay stark on the barren western desert.

The adventurers had been "obliged" to take the old caravan trail out of Celephais, which was a perfectly acceptable route by yak but utter misery on foot. And it was forty miles to the nearest town. Two of those miles had been sufficient to decide the pair against the remaining thirty-eight. As Eldin rightly said: they might as well hang for lions as lambs. Not that they were lambs in any sense of the word; but in any case there were factors to be taken into account other than the blistering desert trek chosen for them by Leewas Nith.

For it was one thing to lose their fine clothes, presented to them by Ilek-Vad's royal tailors—and even worse to be deprived of their yaks—but hardest of all to bear was the loss of their swords. Hero's was a long, light, curved blade of Kled, of exquisite, expensive workmanship and perfectly suited to his hand. Eldin's had been a heavy, straight sword forged in Inquanok, a two-handed blade by dreamland's standards but easily wielded in one hand by this burly son of the waking world.

Moreover, there was something about Eldin's sword, something which would not permit him to leave it in Celephais. It had been touched by the power of the First Ones, which made it very special in Eldin's eyes. Not that the sword appeared to be any different now—it did not seem to have acquired any special powers—but still Eldin felt naked without it and knew no other weapon could ever take its place.

Yes, and there was yet another reason why they must go back. No one high-tailed Eldin the Wanderer and David Hero out of town; not even out of one of dreamland's most beautiful and revered towns. They would yet leave their mark on Celephais. Even a small mark would be better than none at all.

Which was why, as evening came down, they had left the old caravan route and circled back toward the outskirts of the city. They had used whatever cover was available, and their leather clothing, against a background of brown desert and evening shadow, had effectively camouflaged them. Eldin's short-sleeved jacket, shirt and trousers were all dull black, as were his boots, which had been his choice and much to his liking. Hero's clothes were of a russet brown, including his short, hooded cape. Indeed the pair had been lucky to be offered garments so closely matching their habitual dress of old; so that other than their swordlessness, there was now nothing to tell them from the wandering adventurers they had been before reaping the rewards of their heroics in Ilek-Vad.

For however fantastic it had seemed (and despite one or two minor embellishments), Eldin's tale in the court of Leewas Nith had been essentially true, and the pair had more than deserved their rewards. Now, however, penniless once more and outcast, it seemed they must turn again to thievery—at which they were very good—or else starve. And if they were to be thieves, where better to start than with their swords? For without weapons any future escapades seemed more than unlikely, to say nothing of downright dangerous. It may be a bad thing to be caught *in flagrante delicto*, but it is much worse to have to fight your way out with feet, fists and teeth alone!

"Getting dark," Eldin grunted. "Time we were moving."

Hero shook his head. "Uh-uh. Too many lights in the city. And we're too well known there. No, we'll give it another hour or so and let them settle down for the night before we move in. Luckily Ephar Phoog's auction house is near the wharves. The area should be poorly lighted and dressed as we are we'll be near invisible, a couple of ghosts. We should come out of it intact. Then we steal a small boat and put out to sea. After that—" he shrugged. "We'll just have to see which way Lady Luck points us."

"And we'll leave something behind for the folks of Celephais to remember us by, eh?"

Hero looked at his too-eager friend in the dusk. "What would you suggest?" he suspiciously asked.

"Oh, I dunno," Eldin shrugged. "We could always put torch to Ephar Phoog's auction house . . ."

Hero tut-tutted. "You know, I sometimes wonder about you, Eldin," he informed. "Ever since we burned Thalarion you've been dying to set things on fire. First a tavern and now an auction house. But no, I don't think so," he shook his head disapprovingly. "No, I think the theft of a boat quite strong enough. Besides, Celephais is a lovely place. Arson isn't our scene, old friend."

Eldin fell silent for a minute, then grinned through his beard. "They accused the legless firebug of that," he offhandedly informed.

"Eh? A legless firebug?" Hero peered across the gloomy distance separating them from the city. "What did they accuse him of?"

"Too much arson about!" said Eldin with a chuckle.

Hero groaned and cast his eyes heavenward. "At a time like this? How in the name of all that's dreamed can you tell such awful jokes when we're—"

"Oh, don't go on so," growled the older adventurer. "And anyway," he changed the subject, "I'm not so sure you're right."

"Right about what?" asked Hero.

"About staying here for hours on end. I've got the cramps already. Listen, why don't we make our way into the lee of Mount Aran there, and follow the ginkgo trees toward the sea? There'll be no one under those trees tonight but lovers. Also, it'll put us on that side of the city closest to Ephar Phoog's auction house."

Hero looked at Aran where the mountain showed its

snowy cap. Mount Aran was one of those places, of which there were many in Earth's dreamland, that defied Nature's laws. No matter the season, there was always snow on Aran's tall peak. "You're pretty shrewd for all your bad jokes," Hero finally said.

"Good!" grunted Eldin, making to get up. But Hero grabbed his arm before he could stand.

"Half an hour," said the younger man. "It'll be dark enough then. We mustn't jeopardize good planning for unnecessary haste."

Eldin grudgingly grunted his agreement. "Oh, all right," he said. "But I still think we're wasting time."

"Yes, well, better to waste a few minutes here than a year or so in some dungeon under Celephais."

Eldin might have continued the argument had he not noticed the frown suddenly grown on Hero's face and the way his eyes peered at the darkening sky far beyond the city's silhouette of spires, turrets and minarets. "Ah! You've spotted them, have you?" he asked instead.

"Um? Those lights, d'you mean?" said Hero. "What the devil are they?"

"Lights in the sky," Eldin chuckled, "What else?"

"Stars, d'you suppose? They're pretty low in the sky for stars, and they seem to be . . . moving?"

Eldin sighed. "You've never been to Celephais before, have you? This was your first trip here—and you spent most of it looking after me, right?"

Hero nodded, never once taking his eyes from the bright points of light in the sky far beyond the city.

"You know, lad," Eldin went on, "you really should pay more attention when I talk about the things I've done and the places I've seen. Don't you remember when first we decided to come here, how I told you what I knew of Celephais? How Celephais had wonders other than the permanently snowy peak of Mount Aran?"

Hero turned his head to peer into his friend's gloom-shadowed face and frowned in concentration. "Something about ships that sail into the sky?" he hazarded.

Eldin sighed again, this time in resignation. "All right," he said, "we'll start again at square one. Only this time listen:

"Celephais lies in the Valley of Ooth-Nargai. Those hills over there, they're the Tanarians, and the desert behind us is the Oon. Aran you already know; but you don't know about the timelessness."

"Timelessness?" repeated Hero.

Eldin nodded. "Time's queer in the dreamlands, sure enough," he said, "but more so in Celephais. Things don't age greatly here and the seasons don't come around so often. That's one of the reasons, I fancy, why there's always snow on Aran. The whole place seems to resent, to *resist* change.

"And it's this timelessness and continuity that attracted Kuranes to Celephais. He was once a dreamer same as us, but he's gone a ways since then. Still, he's more a benevolent old oracle than a king proper, more a prophet than a power. He spends half his time here in Celephais, the rest of it in Serannian. Now Serannian, that's a really fantastic place!"

"That's what you said about Celephais—before we got here and you started to hit the bottle," Hero grumbled. "Serannian," he tasted the word. "Isn't that the mythical sky-floating city I've heard mention of somewhere?"

"Right," said Eldin, "but it's no myth, I promise you. I've never been there myself, mind you, but according to all the stories I've heard about it—"

"I think it's dark enough now," said Hero.

"Damn me!" Eldin grated. "Even now you haven't been listening, have you?"

"You can tell me later," Hero answered. "We can talk as we go—so long as we keep it quiet. Come on then, let's head for the foot of the mountain. But go carefully whatever you do. Old Leewas Nith wasn't joking when he tossed us out. If we're caught again . . ." And he let the sentence hang.

They cut across the scrub of the desert, moving as shadows, and as they went so Eldin spoke of this marvelous valley and the legends he remembered of it. By the time they reached Aran's foot and climbed it to where the ginkgos waved their fanlike foliage in a light evening breeze, he was telling Hero of the city's fabulous harbor.

"It's said," (he related), "that ships sailing out of the bay of Celephais cease to be governed by the law of gravity. The sea out there," and he nodded his head toward the rolling expanse of ocean beyond the city, "is a funny sort of sea. Normally when you look out to sea the horizon only seems to meet the sky. Here in Celephais it really does! That's why most of the ships that sail from here are bound for Serannian."

"Oh?" said Hero. "Well, that's no damn good to us, is it? I mean what you've said makes Serannian virtually an island. If we end up on—or in—Serannian, it may not be the easiest thing in dreamland to get off again. It would be like leaping out of a frying pan into the fire!"

"Not us," answered Eldin. "We're not heading for Serannian. No, we'll hug the coast and head east. It's only if you make for the horizon that you sail into the sky. There's a coast of clouds up there, piled up by the west wind, and that's where Serannian is built of pink marble."

Hero could not quite hide his snort of derision. "What? I mean, it's bad enough asking me to believe in *any* sort of city in the sky without it being built of marble!"

"The eidolon Lathi's city Thalarion was built of paper," reminded Eldin.

"Yes, it was," Hero agreed, "—on the ground!"

"You know, I often wonder how I ever teamed up with you in the first place," said Eldin. "I can't understand why you're a dreamer at all. You've no imagination, my lad. There's too much of the waking world in you for your own good. After all we've been through, can't you get it into your head that things are different here? Vastly different. Time and space are different, and the laws of Nature and of Science."

"—And of Magic!" Hero added.

"Well, yes, that's true enough," Eldin agreed. "Dream-magic has a certain amount of science in it, and dream-science has more than its share of magic. It's difficult to tell one from the other, really. But anyway, there are mighty engines built into Serannian's foundation. I've heard that they manufacture the ethereal stuff that keeps the city afloat on the air. Perhaps it's this stuff—leaking off, so to speak—that comes drifting down to the sea and changes it. Maybe it forms the great wide river which the traders ride in their galleys from the horizon to the sky."

"Maybe," scowled Hero, a trifle skeptically—too skeptically for his older, more experienced companion.

"Well, you just believe what you want to," Eldin snarled as his patience left him at last. "But remember: the next time you see lights in the sky, don't ask me about them. Right?"

Night-gaunts Over Dreamland

The apparent animosity which existed between the pair meant nothing. Anyone who knew them (though admittedly their true friends could be numbered on two hands and still leave both thumbs and a few fingers to spare) would happily testify that their banter was very often bruising, and especially so on the eve of a grand adventure. It was a matter of nerves, of inner tensions, and on this particular occasion of Eldin's slow emergence from long weeks of drunken misery.

First he had needed to recover from the loss of Aminza Anz, woken up from dreams on the very day when they were to be wed in Ilek-Vad, and now he must recover from the instrument of his recovery. A few days of enforced abstinence while awaiting trial had helped, and with luck the coming escapade might just complete the job. In short, Eldin was "drying out."

As for Hero: he, too, had had a bad time of it. Quite apart from nursemaiding Eldin, what should have been for Hero a luxurious and elysian stay in Celephais had gone disastrously wrong. With their rich robes, money and fine yaks, the pair would have been well advised to play their highest cards—that is, to assume the roles of prosperous merchants and board in one of Celephais' better inns. They had fallen prey to habit, however, and so had put up at the wormy tavern of Arkim Sallai in a less than savory quarter of the city.

There, in an atmosphere reminiscent of other sojourns in dreamland's more earthy inns and taverns, and in the company of shifty characters with questionable backgrounds, they had quickly forgotten their recent and much-applauded heroics and reverted to type. With the almost inevitable result that they were what and where they were now: a pair of fugitives heading through the back streets of Celephais toward Ephar Phoog's auction house ... And also toward a new and no less fantastic adventure than their last, though they could hardly be expected to know that.

They spoke not at all as they moved parallel to the waterfront, traversing the city's shadowed alleys with the supple, alert speed of great cats; and so covert their movements and silent, that a small party of pleasure-seekers which noisily passed them where they merged into the shadows of a shallow shop doorway failed even to suspect their presence. And so at last, completely unchallenged, they arrived at the rear of the auction house, where it was only a matter of moments before they had scaled the high, featureless wall into Ephar Phoog's back yard.

Behind stacks of old chairs and tables and other items of household furniture they found a door with small-paned windows, and here Eldin employed a massive diamond ring (given him by Aminza Anz's father and cleverly retained despite the loss of all else) swiftly to remove one of the near-opaque panes from its frame. Then: a hamlike hand inserted, the bolt drawn, and the auction house standing open to the cat-eyes of the pair where they entered to silently prowl its dusty rooms.

Since their swords were to be auctioned the very next day, they made straight for the auction room itself. Situated centrally in the great house—which was mercifully a warehouse as opposed to a dwellinghouse proper, so that Phoog had his home elsewhere in the city—they found the auction room with its tiers of seats; and here, secure in the knowledge that the light would not be seen from without, Eldin lit a taper.

It was a matter of moments then to find their trusty blades (or "rusty blades," as Hero was wont to have it), and in the glow of the taper they admired the work which some retainer of Ephar Phoog, perhaps the auctioneer himself, had done on the weapons. For from tip to tail the swords had been cleaned, buffed and polished to a high reflectivity, until their razor-edged blades were bright as long, slender mirrors!

"Good swords are rare in dreamland," Eldin breathed, breaking the long silence. "Phoog knows that, and he also knows fine blades when he sees them. These would have fetched a pretty penny, you can bet your life."

"Aye," whispered Hero in answer. "Well, I'm already betting my life—or at least a good part of it—just by being here. So let's get these dear old friends belted on and hustle our backsides out of it, shall we?"

Eldin touched the tip of his nose with a finger and raised a bushy eyebrow. He winked. "Don't be so eager to go," he told his younger companion. "The night is young, after all. You never know what we might find lying about in here if we look closely enough. For instance—" And he pounced on a small crate of four dusty bottles. "Look at this!"

Hero took a square bottle from Eldin, blew the thick accumulation of dust and cobwebs from its squat shape and peered at the ancient label. He whistled.

"Good stuff, is it?" Eldin eagerly asked, licking his lips as he pushed a pair of bottles into his spacious pockets.

"Good? It's the best! Five hundred years old if it's a day. A vintage of primal Sarkomand, by the look of it, and the wines of Sarkomand were known to improve by the century! Here, let me see that ticket on the crate." He ripped the lot card from its string fastenings and read it out loud:

> *"Found in the Hold of a strange*
> *Derelict wrecked on Fang Rocks to*
> *the West of the City of Celephais,*
> *and claimed by Ephar Phoog whose*
> *Retainers seized the Wreck."*

"Well, well, well!"

"Here," said Eldin, "give me that card." He took up a charcoal scribbler from the auctioneer's bench and scrawled on the card's reverse:

> *"Found again in the Auction Rooms*
> *of Ephar Phoog, by Eldin the Wanderer*
> *and David Hero, who, since*
> *they had more Need of it, also*
> *seized it!"*

A few minutes later, after satisfying themselves that there was little else small enough or valuable enough to interest them, the pair left Phoog's premises, both of them chuckling at the thought of the auctioneer's face the next day when he discovered he had been burgled and by whom. "And isn't this better," asked Hero of Eldin, "than simply burning the place down?"

"I suppose you're right," said the older thief. "Certainly we'll attract less attention this way. And all that remains now is our escape from the city . . ."

A pair of shadows once more, they made their way from the auction house to the marble-walled waterfront and quickly chose a vessel. It was a simple little craft, with a single mast folded down and a pair of oars dangling from oarlocks. A tarpaulin covered the prow and forward part of the boat and there was a full cask of water with a tap in the stern. Since they hardly expected to occupy the vessel for more than a night at most, this would seem to be provision enough.

They cast off and rowed quietly for the wall of mist that lay thick on the calm night sea less than one hundred yards from the wharf, but before they could reach it the tarpaulin in the prow was thrown back and a great black-bearded fisherman clasping an empty bottle emerged from a tangle of nets. "Huh? What? Who?" gasped the disoriented man.

"Which? Where? Why?" added Hero speculatively.

Eldin shipped his oar and pointed it at the boat's drunken owner where he staggered about bewildered in the prow. "I know exactly how you feel, lad," he growled. "But tell me, can you swim?"

"Eh? Swim? 'Course I can swim!" came the ale-fuddled answer.

"So swim," said Eldin, and shoved with the oar.

A moment later, leaving a splashing, spluttering swimmer in its wake, their commandeered craft slid into the mist and the dim lights of Celephais' waterfront were soon lost from sight. Now, since there was no wind to speak of, they bent their backs to the oars and pulled into the night, fairly skimming over the mist-wreathed water.

For long minutes they toiled, until suddenly they drew clear of the mist and out onto the open sea. Behind them the harbor lights showed on both sides of the bay's wall of mist, and beyond that rose Mount Aran and the silhouette of Celephaïs, dark now with the exception of a scattered handful of dim lights.

"Safe and sound away," grunted Eldin with a degree of satisfaction. "And is this a breeze I smell? Indeed it is! Up sail, lad, and I'll man the tiller!"

"Aye-aye, Cap'n," said Hero, manhandling the mast into position and rigging the sail. "Which way are we bound, Cap'n, sir?"

"East, lad, along the coast. This here's the Cerenerian Sea, and I've no wish to sail into the sky."

"No, indeed, Cap'n," said Hero, plumping himself down with his back to the mast as Eldin handled the tiller.

"*Brrr!*" shivered the older adventurer where he sat, and he convincingly rattled his teeth.

"Eh?" questioned Hero. "*Brrr*, did you say? Are you cold, old son?"

"Cap'n to you, lad," snapped Eldin, "and damn right I'm cold! Frost on the stars and snow falling, and ice on the lashings to burn a man's hands!"

Now Hero began to frown. Frost, snow, ice? He was still sweating profusely from the hard rowing. "Silly bloody game!" he grumbled.

"No, no!" cried Eldin. "It's cold, I tell 'e! Break out the rum, lad."

"Rum? We've no—" And at last Hero saw his friend's meaning. Laughing, Eldin produced a square bottle and knocked off its neck against the gunwale. He closed his fist round the jagged rim, tilted the bottle and drank through his fingers, then passed the wine to Hero.

"Ah! Great stars of night!" Eldin groaned his appreciation as Hero took a swig in his turn. "And did you ever taste anything like that before?"

"Never!" said Hero, smacking his lips. "But what a waste. This—" he tapped the bottle with a fingernail "—is a wine to be savored in palaces of the gods. A vintage to enhance the flavor of rare viands—not guzzled in a matchstick boat on a midnight sea ... Here, you take this bottle back and I'll crack one of my own!"

And he did ...

Now where hard drinking was concerned Hero and Eldin could normally hold their own with anyone in dreamland. They had boozed and battled their way into and out of at least one quarter of all dreamland's towns and cities, and fully intended to work their way through the other three. This time, however, they were up against the unknown and the unexperienced. Namely, a wine of Sarkomand, matured in the bottle for five long centuries.

Later, when Hero had time to think about it, he would half-remember a similar bout of wine-bibbing in the cavern of Thinistor Udd—and its consequences. He would vaguely recall thinking how exquisitely *smooth* the wine of Sarkomand was in the swallowing, and how he could probably drink a gallon before it caught up with him. Which must have been about fifteen seconds before it caught up with him! Also in the less accessible regions of his mind were kaleidoscope memories of idiot giggling bouts, and coarse, raucous ballads, and of Eldin collapsing with his legs over the tiller, and of the sky going round and round and round and ...

Following which, he remembered the agony of regaining consciousness to thin morning mists, and of lying in the bottom of a boat that rocked and rocked and rocked ... until weak with nausea he lapsed back into his drunken stupor. Then there had been a second wakening, this time to a night sky full of stars which seemed so close that he need only put out his hand to touch them.

And finally there was the present realization that at last it was daylight once more, or very nearly so, and that he was stiff and numb and at last truly awake—the wine burned out of his system, his mouth dry as shredded paper, his eyes burning like hot coals where they gazed up startled from his haggard face into a newly dawning sky—and that the sound of Eldin's groans of misery were sending lances of fire into his skull.

And the knowledge that something had awakened him—had literally shocked him awake—but what?

As if in answer to his unspoken query, the something came again: a great throbbing of leathery wings and a nightmare shape that flapped into view level with the top of the single slender mast. A huge night-gaunt, rubbery and horned, its bared tail seeking purchase on the mast and its prehensile paws grasping at the sail's thin canvas sheet.

"Gaunt!" croaked Hero, leaping (or at least staggering) to his feet—only to be knocked flat a moment later as a second gaunt landed behind him on the port gunwale and buffeted him with its faceless head. For answer to his hoarse-voiced warning Eldin groaned even louder, and Hero might have joined in if his entire being had not already frozen solid.

For he had fallen down with his head and shoulders protruding over the starboard gunwale, which position had served to bring him face to face with the most unexpected and unnerving view of his entire existence in both waking and dream-worlds alike. Far down below the keel of the boat, seen through wispy breaks in a bank of pink and fluffy cloud, the mountains, rivers and angular coastline of dreamland looked like features on a small-scale relief map!

So, instead of groaning, Hero gave a completely uncharacteristic little shriek and hung on desperately to the gunwale as the boat rocked and threatened to tip him into space. And as a flood of adrenalin drove the last dregs of wine from his fevered veins, so the realization dawned on Hero that things had once again gone disastrously wrong.

They were sailing on the Cerenerian Sea in that region of dreamland where the west wind flows into the sky, where cloud-floating, pink-marbled Serannian's incredible bulk is builded on an ethereal shore of clouds. Indeed, they might yet tie up in Serannian's harbor—

—Unless the night-gaunts sank them first!

Man-o'-war

The boat tilted farther yet, until Hero felt himself sliding head first into leagues of sky—but in another moment there came Eldin's grunt of exertion, the whistle of his straight sword slicing air, and the sweet *thwack* of its blade biting deep into rubbery flesh. Then Hero heard his friend's hoarse cry of delight, which almost immediately turned to a croak of alarm as the boat abruptly, violently, rocked back the other way; so violently that Hero was thrown upright against the mast. Feeling his legs under him and steady once more (or nearly so), he drew his sword and sliced at the first alien thing he saw: the half-severed leg of a gaunt where the creature clung to the port gunwale and flapped its mighty bat-wings in a frenzy of agony.

His stroke was good; the curved Kledan steel finished the job Eldin's blade had begun; the gaunt lifted off minus a paw and lower limb and flapped erratically aloft. Hero fancied he could almost hear its screams, and if the thing had had a mouth then certainly he would have heard them. But the crippled gaunt was forgotten in another moment. It was not important. Nothing was important except . . . *where the hell was Eldin?*

Then something heaved and thrashed in the belly of the boat and Hero felt his leg grasped in a steely grip. He gave a great sigh of relief as the heaped nets parted and Eldin emerged red-eyed and roaring. "Gaunt, did you say?" he yelled. "Gaunt? In the singular? Man, there's half-a-dozen of the damned things! I haven't seen such a flock since our little scrap with Thinistor Udd. And that one there—" he pointed with his sword at the lopsided shape that fluttered jerkily in the sky high overhead "—he almost had me overboard . . . Look out, lad—here they come again!"

There were indeed six gaunts in all, including the one they had crippled, and as Hero turned from his companion he saw four of the remaining five come winging in to the attack. As for the fifth—that one was a giant! The biggest gaunt Hero could possibly have imagined, but for all his great size he kept well away from the boat. Hero slitted his eyes in the dawn light and just before the four flyers struck he could have sworn that he saw—a rider? A man or youth, seated well back on the neck of the huge faceless fifth beast. And then—then he was obliged to give all of his attention to more pressing matters. Namely, the attempted wrecking of the stolen boat by these weirdly purposeful gaunts.

No real chance for the adventurers to use their swords now, for the gaunts came at them from below, tilting the boat this way and that with their necks and back in an earnest and dreadfully *urgent* attempt to tip it over. Then one of the rubbery monsters backed off and hurtled in like a dart, its wings folding back at the last moment, to strike the boat such a blow with its arched back that the starboard strakes were stove in. Not only did this action damage the boat but the gaunt too, for following its near-suicidal swoop it rapidly lost height and spiraled down into the cloudbank far below.

"Two down and four to go!" Eldin hoarsely cried as he hastily roped one of his legs to the tiller.

"No, only three," Hero contradicted, hanging onto the wildly swaying mast and waving his curved blade aloft as the specified trio swooped about the wallowing craft, apparently pondering fresh tactics.

"Three?" Eldin queried.

"Yon big fellow has a rider," yelled Hero, "but whoever he is he's a poor general. He commands his troops from the rear. Do you see him?"

"Aye, I see him now," Eldin answered. "Little more than a youth from his looks. But . . . a youth with power over night-gaunts? What in hell's all this about? What's he got against us?"

"Search me," said Hero. "If we can hang on a few minutes more, though, I reckon we'll come out of this in one piece."

"Oh?" yelled Eldin as the three circling gaunts turned inward and came at them in a concerted rush. "And how did you come to that conclusion?"

"It's daylight," cried Hero, slashing at one of the three and causing it to swerve and collide with the mast, which snapped off at its base and was carried off, sail and all. "Gaunts aren't supposed to like daylight."

"You'd better tell them that!" Eldin roared as one of the brutes hit the port strakes such a blow that they shattered inward and showered the pair with splinters of wood.

The boat was obviously done for now. Only the keel held it together where it lay low in the stern and listing badly to port. "This is madness," Hero shouted, gazing wildly and uselessly about. "How the hell do we bail her out?"

"Forget it," Eldin yelled his answer. "Here they come

again—and it seems we've no choice but to go down with out ship!"

They braced themselves for what must be the final assault as the gaunts came at the boat from below. One after the other the hideous creatures hurled themselves at the keel and the bottom strakes, and the boat shuddered and bucked with each fresh strike. It was surely all over now.

Then—

Blinding rays of light stabbed with startling suddenness out of the east, soundlessly seeking out the attacking gaunts where they now flapped and fluttered in a frenzy of terror. The great gaunt and its rider, barely avoiding these raking beams from their as yet unknown source, now veered sharply away across the sky to enter a cloudbank where it lay like so much cotton wool to the west.

The other gaunts immediately followed suit, but as they went one of them was caught by twin beams of brilliant white fire. There was a rasping, rending sound then, and a moment later all that remained of the stricken creature was several tatters of black rubbery stuff, exploding outward and spinning dizzily downward into oblivion.

In a matter of seconds the sky was empty of enemies, and the men in the foundering boat shielded their eyes against the sun which now emerged fully from the clouds to the east. Hero blinked, screwed up his eyes and blinked again, then gasped as he saw a fully-rigged man-o'-war riding the cloud-crests. Sailing directly out of the sun, its decks were lined with the bright mirrors of numerous ray-projectors.

"A warship!" cried Hero. "But what a vessel—a ship of the clouds!"

"A light in the sky," rumbled Eldin, not nearly so elated.

"Hey!" yelled Hero, standing up and waving a strip of sail-cloth at faces which peered down from the railed deck. "By all that's good, take us aboard, lads. Quickly now, or we'll surely go down with our brave little boat . . ."

"Either way, we're sunk," growled Eldin under his breath as the ship gracefully drew alongside.

This time Hero heard him. "Sunk?" he repeated. "Man, we're saved!" But seeing his companion's worried frown, he asked: "How do you mean, sunk?"

"This is one of Kuranes' ships," Eldin explained, "kept in good fighting trim since the Bad Days. He has a great armada of them. Don't ask me what it's doing out here—and I suppose we're lucky to be pulled of this damned hulk anyway—but one thing's certain: we're bound for Serannian."

"And that's bad, eh?" said Hero, grabbing at a rope ladder where it came snaking down from the ship's rail. "Is it worse than falling a couple of miles out of the sky in a cockleshell boat? What's so bad about Serannian?"

"Nothing," grunted Eldin. "It's a beautiful place—except Kuranes is there. He spends his time between Celephais and Serannian, remember?"

Climbing the ladder, Hero said: "So?"

Close behind him Eldin gave an impatient snort. "He's constantly in touch with Celephais," he explained. "They use pigeons. Old Leewas Nith, he might just have told Kuranes all about us."

Hero looked down at Eldin's upturned face. "What? Are we notorious, then? What we did in Celephais wasn't so bad . . . Considering."

"Let's hope you're right," Eldin growled deep in his throat. "But quiet now, they're waiting for us."

As they reached the rail willing hands helped them climb aboard. Too willing, as it transpired, for when at last they stood upon the deck it was without their swords. They had been deftly removed and passed into the hands of members of the ship's crew where they stood behind a uniformed circle of pikemen. The pikes of the latter were all centered upon Eldin and Hero.

"Here, lads," said Eldin in a gruff hurt voice, "is this any way to welcome a pair of fellow sea dogs?" Holding his stomach in from the points of the pikes, he looked askance at his companion.

The pikemen were all small men, but sturdy, and many of them had the aristocratic looks of men of Ilek-Vad. "Who are you?" their commander asked. "And what were you doing out on the Cerenerian Sea in a small boat?"

"Us?" Hero tried his hardest to look innocent. "Why, we're, er, fishermen, of course. Blown off course by a storm—and then attacked by night-gaunts."

"From which you rescued us," added Eldin, "which proves our story."

The commander nodded. "Oh, we rescued you from gaunts, all right—but what's this about a storm?" He frowned. "Why, there's been nought but fair weather for a threemonth!"

Now the vessel's captain came forward, pushing through the pikemen until he faced the newcomers. He was tall for a native of the dreamlands, bearded and keen-eyed. His eyes narrowed now as he stared at the two, and a grin spread slowly across his face. "By all that's—" he began. "Why! It's Eldin the Wanderer and David Hero!" He grasped Hero's hand and pumped it, then thumped Eldin's shoulder with a clenched fist.

Eldin roared delightedly and returned to the punch.

"Look who it is, David!" he cried. "Why, it's old—er—old . . ."

"Dass," the captain prompted him. "Limnar Dass." He smiled broadly and turned to Hero. "Don't you remember me? That fight in the tavern at Barrugas—the way we had to make a run for it?"

"Eh?" said Hero, wildly searching his memory. There had been a good many brawls in a good many places. Finally he said, "Of course we remember you, er, Dass, certainly." But despite his assurance a niggling doubt was growing in the back of his mind. "We remember him, don't we, Eldin?"

"Damn right!" cried Eldin, pummeling the captain's shoulder again for good measure.

But Dass had stopped smiling. "I never saw you in my life before," he coldly stated. "But at least we now know for sure that you are who we thought you were. As for Barrugas: I was never there. Since it's a snake's nest of thieves, however, I was pretty sure that you two would know it—Eldin the Wanderer and David Hero!"

"That was a dirty trick," Eldin snarled, reaching for the captain's throat with hands like great hams. A pike prodded him in the midriff and another lifted to point at his heart.

"Easy, old lad," said Hero softly, his hands tight knots of iron hanging at his sides. "Now is not the time. You're right though—it was a damned dirty trick."

"Perhaps it was," said Dass. "And perhaps I should have made you 'swim,' as you made the owner of your stolen boat! No, no, you two—don't talk to me about dirty tricks. Would you have preferred to stay aboard yon hulk there?" He pointed to the little fishing vessel where it slid slowly downward into clouds, its prow pointing skyward until, gaining speed, it disappeared from view.

"All right," said Hero with a shrug. "As it happens you've done us a favor. And you know all about us. Which only leaves one question. What now?"

Now the captain's grin was an honest one. He looked the pair up and down in open admiration. "You're a couple of cool ones, I'll grant you that," he said. "As for what happens now: you may as well relax, for we won't be in Serannian for another three or four hours yet. And there's only one way off this ship . . . Straight down! I was about to take a meal. Will you join me?"

"Food?" said Hero, realizing how empty his belly felt. "That's not a bad idea."

"What?" cried Eldin. "Eat? With a dog who'd play that sort of dirty trick on me? Not likely!"

Dass shrugged, took Hero's arm and began to turn away. "Hold!" growled Eldin; and more quietly: "What's on the menu?"

"Duck," said Dass, "with small potatoes and green peas. And liqueurs and brandy from Iztar-Iln."

"Brandy?" Eldin's mouth watered.

"Aye," Dass nodded. "Not so fiery as the brandy of the waking world, they tell me, but good for that. Well, are you coming? Or would you prefer good bread and cheese with the pikemen, and a cup of strong green tea to wash it down?"

Eldin considered for a moment, then said: "I accept your apology!"

Leading them to his quarters, Captain Limnar Dass chuckled inwardly at the style of these two rogues. He wasn't sure why King Kuranes wanted to see them, but he would find it a great pity if they were to be punished too harshly. He liked their cut. The dreamlands could do with a few more like these two—

But only a few . . .

City in the Sky

While Hero and Eldin enjoyed the captain's company, food and drink, above decks a pigeon was taken from its basket and a message inserted into the tiny cylinder attached to its leg; and while yet the adventurers sipped their liqueurs, the bird was airborne over the ship's billowing red sails and winging for Serannian. Thus it was that as the man-o'-war breasted the cloud-crests for port—which was still distant by more than a good hour's sailing—knowledge of its coming, and of the passengers it carried, passed into the hands of King Kuranes.

This was not the first communication the King had received in respect of the two men aboard the man-o'-war. Indeed, over the past twenty-four hours there had been three such messages. This was the first, however, from one of the three ships Kuranes had sent out to search the Cerenerian Sea for a small fishing boat, that same craft stolen by Hero and Eldin in Celephais . . .

As for the other messages: they had all been from Leewas Nith. The first had been in the form of the magistrate's weekly report of court proceedings, in which the case of Eldin the Wanderer and David Hero was given brief mention; the second had been to report certain matters of burglary, assault and piracy, which crimes had also allegedly involved the same pair of adventurers; and the third had been a wordy report which told a most strange and astounding tale.

For it seemed that following the enforced exit of the pair from Celephais, proof of their fantastic claims had begun to trickle in. Merchants from Ilek-Vad had brought stories from the court of Randolph Carter himself, where recently a most unlikely pair of rogues had been royally entertained as reward for deeds away and beyond any call of duty. Also, word had arrived from Theelys on the River Tross, where the good wizard Nyrass had his castle. The word was that two men and a girl had flown a huge leaf into Nyrass' gardens, and that now a Great Tree was growing there.

Fantastic stories were echoing across the dreamlands from all quarters, tales which seemed to corroborate the many things Eldin the Wanderer had told Leewas Nith in the main courtroom of Celephais. And so the High Magistrate had set about to correlate these many small pieces of information, including what he remembered of Eldin's seemingly boastful narrative. Except that the Wanderer's story no longer seemed quite so boastful.

Eldin had maintained that he and David Hero were real heroes. Now, from what Leewas Nith could see of it, it appeared that they were indeed. In which case he had wronged them—if only a little. If they had been feted when first they arrived in Celephais, then none of this would have happened. If he, Leewas Nith, had known of their heroics sooner . . . If, if, if!

Too late now, but nevertheless he finished piecing together their recent history and sent it, via carrier pigeon, to Kuranes in Serannian. As to why he told his King the whole story: that is easily answered. If a sailor sets out

from Celephais across the Cerenerian, unless he knows
that sea most intimately, then surely will he sail into
those regions where the sea meets the sky, where
gravity-defying Serannian is builded upon an ethereal
shore of clouds.

As for Kuranes himself: he had paid little heed to the
first two notes. There were plenty of rogues in the
dreamlands and these men from the waking world
seemed to be just a couple more. Besides, he had other
things on his mind, problems which troubled him
sorely.

But on receipt of the third message an irresistible
idea had occurred to Kuranes. Here was he, seeking an
answer to a momentous problem—one which may well
affect all the lands of Earth's dreams in their entirety—
and somewhere out on the Cerenerian Sea, at this very
moment, the answer he sought might well be drifting
with the aerial tides . . . in the shape of a couple of cut-
purses whose origins lay in the waking world. Well, and
why not? Kuranes himself was once a waking-worlder,
though he had been known by a different name then.
Yes, and Randolph Carter, too, the King of Ilek-Vad.

And yet again Kuranes read Leewas Nith's minus-
cules, which told the tale of the two as the High Magistrate of Celephais had finally pieced it together. If
only half of it were true, then indeed these men were
heroes!

Apparently their adventures had started in Theelys
and had taken them to the source of the Tross in the
Great Bleak Range of mountains. There, they had destroyed the evil sorcerer Thinistor Udd; not to mention
an avatar of the dark demon god Yibb-Tstll, in the
shape of a hideous stone idol which walked at Thinistor's command. There too had they rescued Aminza

Anz, darling of Ilek-Vad and long-stolen from that fair city by the sorcerer's gaunts.

Moreover, they had climbed a great Keep of the First Ones, with the result that all three of them (for Aminza Anz went with them) had then set out upon a grand quest across all the lands of Earth's dreams. During their ensuing adventures they had ridden a raft for end-less leagues through nighted bowels of earth, and the life-leaf of a Great Tree across the dawn skies of dream-land; they had burned demon-cursed Thalarion to the ground and gathered up three stolen Wands of Power; and finally they had returned to the keep in the moun-tains to free the sleeping First Ones from eons of en-forced slumbers.

All of these and other wonders the men from the waking world had performed, and now . . . ? Perhaps Kuranes could find something else for them to do. He must give the matter some very serious thought . . .

Kuranes was still thinking things over when the man-o'-war of Captain Limnar Dass sailed into Serannian's har-bor and moored at a quay of blood-hued marble. Since the day was already half-spent he had decided against giving the adventurers audience until the evening, and between times Captain Dass could entertain them.

Which was why, when Dass and his—guests?—came down the gangplank onto the quayside, Kuranes' special courier was there to meet them and hand the captain a message in the King's hand. After reading the King's note, Dass turned a speculative eye upon the adventur-ers.

"Seems I'm to look after you for few hours longer," he told them. "The King won't see you till tonight."

"Is that bad?" asked Hero.

Dass shrugged. "Normally you'd be handed over to

the peacekeepers," he said, "and eventually you'd be tried. On this occasion—" he paused and frowned.

"Well?" growled Eldin.

"It's just that it's so unusual for Kuranes himself to sit in judgment," Dass answered. "Tell me, apart from your boat-stealing activities and all, what else have you two been up to?"

"Nothing much," Eldin airily answered. "A bit of spirited boozing, some brawling." He looked at Hero sideways. "A little womanizing."

Hero returned his look with a snort. "Not to mention a spot of arson about!" he said.

"Hmm," mused Dass. "Well, it seems to me that none of that is really worthy of Kuranes' personal attention. P'raps there's something you've forgotten to mention . . . Anyway," he quickly went on, changing the subject, "what would you say to an air-bath?"

"A what?" asked Hero.

Dass grinned. "Come on, I'll show you."

As they made from the quayside and into the streets of the amazing aerial city proper, Eldin cast furtive eyes all about, taking in everything he saw. There were no pikemen now, just Eldin, Hero, and the man-o'-war's captain. Dass spotted his covert squirming—both physical and mental—and said:

"Whatever it is you're thinking about, Eldin—or thinking of thinking about—I'd better warn you now that it's probably unthinkable."

Hero looked at his companion's scowling face and asked: "Were you thinking things, old lad? Well, I reckon Dass is right. I've had a few thoughts myself and they all lead me to one conclusion. There's simply no way off this airborne rock, so we'd just better face up to what we've got coming. Dass," he turned to the captain, "Where's this air-bath of yours?"

"In here," smiled Dass, ushering them in through an arched doorway from which issued copious clouds of scented steam. He tossed a golden triangular tond to a man in a crimson towel where he sat behind a desk of moisture-slick marble, then led the way through a second archway to where an attendant in a green towel loomed suddenly out of hot banks of steam to confront them.

The attendant waited until (not without a great deal of grumbling and grousing on Eldin's part) they had all three shed their garments to stand pink and naked; and then, gathering up their discarded clothing, he guided them to a huge stone table studded with massive iron staples. From each staple there hung a great length of light but extremely strong chain. Here the three were given wide leather belts to fasten about their waists, to each of which the attendant attached the loose end of a chain.

They were now firmly secured to the table, and when the attendant was satisfied that their fastenings were safe he led all three of them forward through the steam to a rim of marble where the floor fell away into billowing clouds of exotically perfumed, rose-tinted vapors. Many other lengths of chain disappeared downward into this great cauldron, jangling and rattling against its slippery marble lip.

"When we're done," Dass explained, "our clothes will have been spruced up for us and we'll all feel like new men."

"Oh?" Hero chuckled. "Well, of course you two can suit yourselves, but as for me—I'll settle for a new woman!" He slapped Eldin on the shoulder and the two roared with laughter.

While this was going on Dass positioned himself behind them. Now, as they suddenly sensed his intention and turned toward him, he stepped forward and gave them each a push, so that they skidded on the slippery surface before sliding over the curved lip and into the rolling vapor-clouds. As they went they managed to grab hold of each other, so that they were not separated as they whirled in air and moisture-laden cloud.

For a second or two the pair were too stunned to utter a sound, too shocked even to think, but as it dawned on them that there was no sensation of falling—that indeed they were suddenly weightless and that no danger threatened—so they relaxed and began to enjoy the invigorating experience of being suspended in air and washed by hot, spicy, billowing vapors. Dass, too, had entered the "pool," and he quickly made his way to where the pair floated at the ends of their chains.

"How do you do that?" asked Hero breathlessly as Dass emerged from opaquely swirling walls of vapor, his arms and legs sculling like the limbs of some great frog. "Are you swimming?"

"Yes," answered Dass with a grin. "It's not as fast as water swimming, but you get there in the end." He turned on his back, placed his hands under his head and closed his eyes. "I'm for a nap," he informed. "You'd be advised to do the same. About an hour from now the sprays will wake us up."

"Sprays?" Eldin repeated him. "What sprays?"

"Hot and cold water sprays that hit you from all sides, so that you don't know whether to freeze or fry," Dass answered. "Very uplifting . . ." And he drifted off to sleep.

Now the adventurers began to experiment, twisting this way and that and hauling themselves along their chains. Delighted with the weird sensation of weightlessness, Eldin said, "Why, it's like a free–fall sauna!"

"A what?" questioned Hero, equally exhilarated.

"Something from the waking world," said Eldin with a frown as vague, half-glimpsed memories faded back into forgotten regions of his mind. "I think."

They played and floundered and fell about like fools for a few minutes more until, from close at hand, suddenly they heard female voices chattering and giggling. Now the pair twisted about until they faced each other with widening eyes. Women? Girls used the air-baths too? Mixed bathing? In the nude?

The sight of Eldin imitating a great frog was more than Hero could bear. He doubled with laughter as his burly companion went sculling away into the billowing vapors; but a few moments later, as Eldin's uproarious chortling reached back to him intermingled with the delighted *Oohs* and *Aahs* and coy giggles of a dozen girlish voices . . .

"That's a neat trick," said Hero much later, as they dined in a restaurant that looked out over the Cerenerian Sea. "The air-bath, I mean. How's it done, Limnar? How do they suspend you like that in the mid-air?"

"Shh!" Dass answered. "Just sit still for a minute and listen . . . There, do you hear it?"

"I hear it," said Eldin, nodding. "I've been hearing it ever since we stepped off your ship onto the quayside. A deep down throbbing and humming. What does it mean?"

"Those are the mighty engines that manufacture the essence which keeps Serannian afloat," Dass explained. "And the air-baths—they were built above the vents where the city's engineers blow the stuff off. As its potency wanes, so it's vented. Add a mixture of steam and a few exotic scents—"

"Amazing!" said Hero. "And you were right. So invigorating, so refreshing—"

"So *sexy*!" Eldin interrupted. "All those girls."

"Ahem!" said Dass. "Yes, well, you're not really supposed to go cavorting with the females, Eldin."

"Oh, I don't know," answered the Wanderer. "What say you, David?"

Hero looked up with a broad smile on his face. "The air-baths were a lot of fun, Limnar," he said, "but you can keep them for me. I'll settle for a good cavort any old time!"

The Curator

"Since we're on this side of Serannian," said Dass as they left the restaurant, "and since we've an hour or so to spare before the Tilt, I suggest we visit the Museum."

"You know, Limnar," Eldin sighed after a moment's thought, "I've somehow grown to like you—despite the fact that you constantly speak in riddles! What, pray tell, is the Tilt?"

"And what," Hero added, "has it to do with our seeing Kuranes?"

"Transport problems in Serannian," Dass began by way of explanation, "are nonexistent. We have bicycles, and we have the Tilt. Serannian's surface is more or less flat, or would be under normal circumstances. But four times a day everything is downhill . . ." He paused and smiled as if to say, "there you have it."

"Good!" cried Eldin when it became apparent that Limnar had said his all. "Excellent! Clear as bloody mud!"

Hero looked deep into the captain's eyes but found no trace of humor there. Since Dass was obviously sincere, the fault must lie elsewhere. "Would you like to say all of that again?" he invited. "Only—could you possibly put it some other way?"

"One we can understand," Eldin added.

Dass sighed. "The sky-island has a built-in tilt," he said. "Not a big one, but a tilt nevertheless. We call it *the* Tilt. It travels clockwise and completes a circuit every six hours. Therefore, four times a day you can cycle downhill, right across the city if you wish."

"Hmm," mused Hero. "Yes, I'd noticed that."

"Eh?" said Eldin, mouth agape. "Noticed what? How come you always notice things after the fact?"

"The bikes," Hero answered. "Lots of bikes, but all going in one direction. And none of them have pedals!"

"Of course not," said Dass. "By the time you've spent an hour or two in any one place, it's usually time to ride the Tilt home again! Why pedal when in a couple of hours you can freewheel? Anyway, don't worry about it. After we've had a look at the Museum you'll be able to experience the Tilt for yourselves. Kuranes' manor house is on the other side of the city, so we'll have to bike it."

"His manor house?" queried Eldin. "Not a palace?"

Dass grinned in a manner the adventurers were becoming used to. "No," he shook his head. "Oh, he's King, right enough, but he styles himself Lord. Lord of Ooth-Nargai, Celephais, and the sky around Serannian. He was once a waking-worlder, remember? Old habits die hard."

The adventurers stared at each other for a moment, then Hero turned back to Dass. "It's a funny old place, your Serannian," he said. "But tell me, Limnar, what makes you think we'd be interest in.... a museum, did you say?"

"*The* Museum, yes. Follow me." He led them down an alley to the sea wall, then pointed across the cloudbank sea to where a great circular structure was perched on a promontory at the eastern extreme of the sky-island. Beneath the circular building the rock was a shallow crust less than fifty feet thick, and beneath that—nothing.

Eldin frowned. "Captain Dass," he said, reverting to the formal, "that seems a damned strange place to build a museum. Why, it looks ready to break off and fall into the sky!"

"*The* Museum," Dass insisted. "Oh, it's safe enough. Indeed, that's the whole idea—safety. There's only one way into the Museum, you see, and that's along the causeway over the neck of the promontory. One way in and one way out. Thieves think twice before they tackle the Museum. That's why I thought you'd like to see it. Give your imagination something to work on. Take your minds off your interview with Kuranes. Oh, yes, the Museum would be a hard place to crack, all right—but the Curator, impossible!"

"Yes, well, you've lost me again," said Hero. "I mean, we're talking about a museum . . . all right," he quickly held up his hands, "*the* Museum—a place of mummies and bones and books and—"

"Gems and jewels and precious stones," said Dass. "And golden figurines, ivory statues, jade miniatures; and priceless antiques, works of art and—"

"Whoa!" cried Eldin. "Hold on a minute. All of that? In there?" And he leaned on the sea wall and nodded his head toward the building on the promontory. Dass grinned as he noticed the gleam in the older adventurer's eye. In Hero's eyes, too.

"Jewels?" said the younger man in a dry voice. "Gold?"

"That's right," said Dass. "I guessed you'd be interested. Come on then. It's closer than it looks. A ten-minute walk, that's all . . ."

The causeway was narrow, walled, and perhaps thirty yards in length. Since there was room for only two abreast, the three men had to cross single file in order to allow sightseers leaving the Museum the right of passage. Looking down over the low wall as they went, Eldin and Hero were able to gaze almost straight down into uncounted fathoms of air—the aerial "deeps" of the Cerenerian Sea—beneath which the cites, towns, lakes, rivers, mountains and less extraordinary seas of Earth's dreamland were spread like some fantastic miniature world which reached to the horizon. Far off they could even see Celephais, clearly recognizable where snow-capped Aran's white head was raised before the nearby Tanarians.

"Hardly the place for a walk on a windy day," Hero dryly commented as fleecy clouds scudded by beneath his feet.

They entered the Museum through a great archway and found themselves in a three-storied building of stone whose sealed windows were of unbreakable crystal. Ventilation was through the archway, which had no door, and also through a square aperture in the ocean-facing curve of the wall which was big as a large window but placed much higher. Its sill was all of five feet from the floor, so that when the adventurers stood on tiptoe, they were just able to stick their heads out to look down over the sky-island's very rim.

Though the Museum had three stories, the first and second floors contained only those items with which ordinary museums commonly concern themselves: Hero's "mummies and bones and books," and suchlike. The visitors opted to remain on the ground floor, however, for this was where the museum's valuables were housed—of which the quantity and quality were utterly beyond belief.

"Strangely," said Eldin, pausing before an open cabinet of cut rubies as big as pigeon's eggs, "I feel a sort of affinity with this place. Curious, eh?"

"What's strange or curious about it?" asked Hero. "You're a damned thief, right? And this place is crammed with goodies!"

"No, it's not that," Eldin answered with a frown, "though granted I do find these baubles attractive. No, it's something else, but I don't quite know what. I rather fancy I must have been an erudite, scholarly sort of chap in the waking world. A haunter of museums or some such."

"Is that right?" said Hero, frowning a pseudo-serious frown. "Well, perhaps you'd tell me, learned haunted one, if you've noticed anything else strange about this place?"

"Hmm?" Eldin cocked his head on one side.

"There's no security," said Hero. "These treasures— why, we could just walk right out of here with them! It completely contradicts what our good friend here, Captain Limnar Dass, told us."

"I told you the Museum was safe," said Dass. "And so it is. You'd know what I meant if you could see the Curator. But you probably won't. He's here somewhere, but very rarely seen. Usually he only puts in an appearance if someone tries to steal something."

"But how could the Curator know?" asked Hero.

Dass shrugged. "He always does," he answered.

"Something else!" cried Eldin, snapping his fingers. "I knew something was puzzling me. There are no labels, notes, histories of the exhibits. There *are* exhibits—" he licked his lips "—indeed there are—but nothing to tell us anything about them."

"Only the fact," said Dass, "that everything is very rare, very beautiful, or very precious. I'll tell you what I know of the Curator, if you wish; not that it amounts to a lot, but—"

But at that moment, coming toward them through a crowd of visitors from a dozen different regions of the dreamlands, Dass spied a small whiskered man dressed in the livery of the waking world. "Ah!" the captain said. "One of the King's retainers. It looks like Kuranes has finally sent for you."

The captain was right. The whiskered man introduced himself as Lord Kuranes' No. 3 Butler, and he asked Dass and his wards to go at once to the manor house. They followed him out under the stone archway and onto the causeway, but halfway across there was someone—some*thing*—waiting for them. Something which brought them to an abrupt halt.

The Curator was vaguely manlike, thin, tall, spiky, lumpy, shiny and tough-looking, many-armed, and he had glittering crystal eyes. He was built of metal, which was rather noisy when he moved, but apart from that he was silent. He was silent now as he confronted Kuranes' butler, Dass and the two adventurers.

"Now what's all this about?" wondered Hero out loud as the gangling metal being clanked to one side and let the butler pass.

"Perhaps he's been somewhere and only just returned?" Dass suggested.

"No," said Hero through clenched teeth, his eyes narrowing as he turned them on Eldin where he had fallen back to bring up the rear. "No, I think he's here on business—but not with you and me."

As if in agreement with the younger adventurer's

words, the metal man once more stood aside to let first Dass, then Hero pass; but when a rather pale Eldin shuffled forward, the Curator clankingly blocked the way. His crystal eyes glittered palely and faint beams of light flickered of the Wanderer's drawn face. From somewhere deep inside Eldin managed to summon up a mirthless grin. He tried to squeeze past the Curator . . .

Quick as thought the robot shot out incredibly thin arms to lift Eldin clear of the causeway and hold him out over the wall. Looking straight down, Eldin saw clouds scudding by, and far below them a shore of dreamland washed by gently foaming waves. Knowing he was about to be dropped, the Wanderer sought for words with which to protest his end. They stuck in his tinder-dry throat, unspoken, as on the causeway Hero hurled himself upon the Curator's flank.

"Damn you, you metal dog!" he cried. "If you drop him, I swear I'll see to it that you rust in some ferrous metal hell!"

The Curator said nothing, but one of his many metal arms grasped Hero by the hair and shoved him out to arm's length, lifting him until he danced on tiptoe. With Hero held in this painful position, Eldin was brought back from eternity and set down upon the causeway. Weakly he leaned against the wall as the Curator pointed a metal hand at his jacket pocket.

"Yes, you're right, damn you!" Eldin gasped, and with a trembling hand he took out a single large ruby and held it up. Now the Curator released Hero and pointed back across the causeway to the Museum. People made way as Eldin turned and walked unsteadily back to the archway and beneath it, with the Curator clanking along behind him.

Hero made to follow but Dass stopped him. "Your large friend is lucky," he said breathlessly. "The Curator has been known to kill would-be thieves outright—out of hand. And you may be sure your threat didn't worry him. I doubt if he even heard or understood it."

They waited on the causeway like a pair of pariahs while the rest of the Museum's visitors hurriedly departed, and in a few seconds Eldin reappeared and joined them. He turned back to stare into the shadows under the archway, where now the bizarre figure of the Curator silently stood, his crystal eyes full on the three.

Eldin shuddered involuntarily. "If ever he lays eyes on me again," he said, "he'll kill me. And I'm sorry but ... I think the same goes for you two. He didn't say so—said nothing—but I got that impression."

"Oh?" snarled Hero as he and Dass ushered Eldin over the causeway. "And what did we do to annoy him?"

"You were with me," the Wanderer answered. "That's enough."

"Eldin," Limnar Dass softly called when they were off the causeway and safely out of sight of the Museum. As Eldin turned toward him he continued: "Never do anything like that again, not in my company. For if you do—big man as you are—I swear I'll knock your head off!"

"I'm a thief," growled Eldin. "I couldn't resist it."

"Next time—if ever there is one—resist it," Dass advised. "It certainly won't help your cause where Kuranes is concerned. His No. 3 Butler, who by now will be halfway to his master's manor house, is bound to tell him."

They found a railed square where several bikes were parked near shrubs and fountains. The bikes had engaged/vacant indicators set centrally on their handlebars. They took three vacant bikes and set off, Limnar Dass leading, straight across the sky-island and through the inner streets of the city. Vague memories lingered, of bike-rides in the waking world; and so the adventurers soon got used to free-wheeling and their riding quickly became less wobbly and erratic as they rode the Tilt through Serannian.

Half an hour later, leaving the busier streets behind them and coming out into the suburbs on the western side of the city, the two adventurers drew level with Limnar Dass and after a while the captain began to talk to them. His friendly grin told them that Eldin's instinctive thievery was forgiven—by him at least. This prompted the Wanderer to ask:

"Limnar, about the Museum and its Curator: what's it all about? I mean, that's no ordinary museum, and as for the Curator—"

"Both the Museum and the Curator have been here since long before Serannian. Ever since there was a sky-island. What he is and why he brought his collection here, nobody knows. There are theories, of course, but no one knows for sure. He does no harm—within certain limits—and the Museum does contain many marvelous things. Kuranes goes there often . . ."

"And speaking of Kuranes," said Hero ominously as he spied an ivied tower rising above the distant copse, "that must be his manor house. Right?"

"Correct," answered Dass, and he sensed the tenseness of the pair. "Listen," he said, "if you're thinking of making a run for it, forget it. There's nowhere to run."

After a moment of silence, Hero answered: "Don't worry, we can take what's coming to us."

"Good! But let's make a little more speed, shall we? Evening's drawing in and I do believe it's going to rain." He put his feet down onto the cobbled lane and urged his bike ahead into deepening gloom. Overhead, lowering clouds opened and the evening's first raindrops came pattering down . . .

Kuranes' Quest

They rode through great iron gates into a large-cobbled courtyard, at the back of which stood the manor house itself, with its tower of gray stone rising above. Mist swirled in ghostly tendrils from gardens of ancient, ivy-grown oaks and green-shining shrubbery. The rain was falling steadily now, so that the three were almost glad to hand over their bikes to a squad of pikemen before venturing into the stone-flagged entrance hall.

Perhaps "venturing into" gives the wrong impression; in fact they were guided into the hall at the gleaming points of a half-dozen pikeheads. At least, Hero and Eldin were. Limnar Dass went of his own accord.

Inside, a fire roared in an open fireplace, with Kuranes' No. 3 Butler standing close by. He beckoned to Dass and offered him a chair by the fire, but at sight of Hero and Eldin—especially the latter—his nose went up in the air and his back visibly stiffened. A man of Celephais or Ilek-Vad he most certainly was, but he played the part of an English butler extraordinarily well.

"Tattletale!" Eldin hissed at him over his shoulder as the pikemen warily prodded him and his younger companion on down the length of the hall toward heavy, oak-paneled doors. The doors swung silently open at their approach and they passed through, but the pikemen remained behind in the entrance hall. Two more whiskered, liveried butlers—doubtless Nos. 1 and 2—were waiting within to close the doors and bow to the pair, however superciliously. Not to be outdone, Hero and Eldin followed suit. For their pains they were directed down a narrow strip of green carpet across the huge, high-ceilinged room to where a lone figure sat at a desk so massive that it utterly dwarfed him.

This was Kuranes, who now called out, "Come forward, you two. Please come forward."

"Eldin," whispered Hero to his bulky companion as they moved to obey, "this man is no mere magistrate. What we say to him can make or break us. That's if we're not already broken. So let's keep it very polite, right?"

"Right," Eldin whispered back. "Damn it, David, I wish I hadn't tried to lift that ruby. But if only I'd managed it, eh? Why, we'd have lived like kings for five years on that one stone!"

"We still will live like kings," Hero answered out of the corner of his mouth, "if we get out of this intact," With a nervous grin he added: "You're not the only thief in Earth's dreamland, you know . . . and by no means the best!"

"*What?*" Eldin gasped. "D'you mean to tell me that—"

"*Shh!*" hissed Hero. "It'll keep."

They marched the last few paces in line and came to a halt, with a little less than military precision, before Kuranes' desk. And now the Lord of Serannian gazed steadily, curiously at them where they stood, while they in turn looked back at him.

Slightly built but regally robed, gray-bearded but

bright-eyed, Kuranes wore the unmistakable characteristics of a waking-worlder. There was that *realness* about him which set him apart—as it did all men of the waking world—from the indigenous denizens of Earth's dreamland. It was there in his voice, too: that thrilling reminder of days long forgotten, days spent in lands *outside* or higher than the so-called subconscious.

"So you are the men of whom I've recently heard so much, are you? A pair of brawlers, braggarts and thieves. And you—" he turned piercing eyes upon Eldin, "you even dared to bring your thieving habits into Serannian!"

"My Lord," Eldin uncomfortably began, "I—"

"Hear me out," Kuranes held up his hand. "I will list the crimes of which you have been accused—both of you—since your arrival in Celephais right up to the present moment. When I am done I will ask if you are innocent or guilty. You will answer, with one word, and then we shall see what we shall see. Agreed?"

Hero wordlessly nodded, Eldin less certainly.

Quickly their sins tripped off Kuranes' tongue, his voice empty of emotion, his eyes staring first at Hero, then Eldin, then back to Hero, until he was done. He missed nothing out, and Eldin's worst fears were realized when the attempted theft of the great ruby brought the King's catalog of their crimes to a conclusion. Now Kuranes leaned back in his great chair and tapped the top of his desk with his fingernails.

"Well?" he said. "Are you innocent? . . . Or guilty?"

"I—" began Eldin.

"Guilty," Hero growled it out low, cutting his companion short.

Eldin gritted his teeth but held his head up high. "Aye," he said, "guilty. Me especially."

"Very well," said the King after a moment's pause.

"And now I must decide what to do with you. Criminals you are, but I've yet to meet a criminal who is all bad . . . or have I?" And he gazed at Eldin. "Let it pass—there are things on your side." He stood up and walked round the great desk, his scarlet, gold-hemmed dressing gown belling with his movement.

Now he steepled his hands, turned his back on the pair and began to pace the floor. "You are dreamers," he said, "or at least you were. We cannot call you dreamers when you ar no longer able to wake up! Men once of the waking world, then, who now abide in dreams. Well, there we have something in common at least. That's a point in your favor. Some of my best friends were once waking-worlders . . .

"Also," the King eventually went on, "You are brave men. I could have you thrown in jail—indeed, I could have you hurled down from Serannian's rim!—which you must know. And knowing it, still you admitted your guilt. I suppose it could be argued that failing to do so would have been to condemn yourselves, for of course I *know* you are guilty of many of the charges. Still, I note that none of your accusers call you liars. You bend the truth occasionally, perhaps often, but you do not seem to lie harmfully. Not that I have been able to discover.

"Furthermore, you are daring. To attempt to steal from the Museum—that was to be daring to the point of reckless! I would hate to think that your daring springs from sheer foolishness . . ." He stopped pacing, faced them squarely, frowned, and finally nodded; and they saw that he had made up his mind about something.

"The choice shall be yours," Kuranes said at last. "To be transported back to Celephais and there remain for five years in one of Leewas Nith's dungeons . . . Or—"

"Or?" urged Hero, when the pause grew so long as to be unbearable. "You were about to say, your Majesty?"

"You have qualities—should we call them skills?—which I can use," said Kuranes. "As my agents you would have my protection, access to the means at my disposal—eventually my pardon."

"Your agents?" said Hero, frowning.

Kuranes nodded. "There's a quest I would have you undertake," he said.

"A quest!" cried Eldin. "Why, we're your men, Sir—for there never were questers like Eldin the Wanderer and Hero of Dreams!"

"The dangers may well be terrific," warned Kuranes.

"We laugh at danger." Eldin assumed what he supposed to be a rakish pose.

"There will be no reward other than a pardon for your past crimes," said the King.

"What more could we wish for than to do the King's work?" asked Hero, wide-eyed and innocent.

"The quest will set you against powers which could destroy your immortal souls, let alone your subconscious minds. There's black wizardry involved, demonic horror, nightmares which only a madman could dream, and—"

"Whoa!" cried Eldin. "Er, excuse me, Lord, but are you trying to enlist us or unman us? Damn me, five years in old Leewas Nith's dungeons are beginning to sound like a veritable holiday!"

Kuranes nodded. "Well they might," he agreed, "but as I said before, the choice is yours."

"Can't you tell us more about this quest of yours?" asked Hero. "Before we make up our minds?"

Kuranes shook his head. "You make your decision now," he answered.

"Then we have no option," Eldin growled. "We accept."

Hero nodded. "Aye," he said, "we're your men. We'll go questing for you, Lord Kuranes."

Now Kuranes sighed a great sigh and it was as if a huge weight had been lifted from his shoulders. "Very well. Now come, sit down. Have you eaten? No matter, you could manage a leg of chicken, I'm sure. And a glass of wine? Good!" He clapped his hands and the butlers, who had approached as the three took their seats at the great desk, bowed and left the room through a door in a curtained alcove.

In a few moments they were back with a tray of chicken joints, a bottle of wine and three glasses. When they had served the King and his guests, they retired to the ends of the huge desk where they remained, motionless, like guardsmen at the gates of a palace. Kuranes' appetite was good as he tucked into his evening repast; but the two adventurers, already well fed, merely picked at their meat and sipped a little wine as they waited for him to have done.

Finally, dabbing at his lips with a handkerchief, he sat back and gazed afresh at the pair. "Let me first tell you," he began, "what is likely to happen if your work for me is not successful. Can you picture Serannian, the entire sky-island, sinking into the Cerenerian Sea, picking up speed, breaking into pieces as it crashes to the world below? And all those thousands of people, screaming as they tumble through space, crushed by falling masonry—bursting like plums as the city slams down into oblivion!"

Hero and Eldin looked at each other with raised eyebrows for a moment, then the younger man turned back to Kuranes and asked: "And is that it? We're to go questing for a means to save Serannian? Fair enough.

But surely, before there's an effect there's a cause. What makes you think the sky-island is doomed? You've hinted that the threat is of a supernatural nature. Well, then, what's its source?"

Kuranes nodded in a satisfied manner and smiled a faint smile, the first his guests had seen upon his face. "Good!" he said, and again it was as if a weight had left his shoulders. "Those are some of the questions I would expect from questers who know their business. Very well, let's get down to it. What do you know of Zura?"

"Zura?" answered Eldin. "Why, yes, I know of it. It's a place, a land, a forbidden spot beyond Thalarion. Certain phrases spring to mind, meaningless phrases heard in connection with the place. 'The Charnel Gardens of Zura,' for instance, and 'Zura's Dead Legions.' Traders have always avoided Zura and cartographers usually leave it off their maps. In fact, if you talk about Zura in the healthier lands of Earth's dreams, why, you pretty soon end up talking to yourself! In short, it's a bad place."

"Indeed it is," Kuranes agreed, "and yet—that's where you're going!"

There was a long pause before Hero, who had also heard of Zura, said: "Just like that?"

"Basically, yes," answered Kuranes. "Oh, there are more details—you need to know why you're going there, for one thing—but essentially the trick is to get you into Zura, discover a certain something, then get out again and return to Serannian."

Slowly Eldin stood up, his huge knuckles white on the top of the great desk, his face darkening. "Lord Kuranes," he said, "your offer to work boils down to this: five years in a dungeon or certain death! You must thing we're as daft as you are!"

"You speak treason!" snapped the butlers in unison,

springing forward and coming upon the pair from the flanks.

"He most certainly does," agreed Hero as he jumped to his feet. He placed his back against Eldin's so that they faced Kuranes' angry, whiskered retainers. "Speaks it fluently, and several other tongues—including horse-sense. But now and then he's a bit hasty, that's all." To Kuranes, speaking very quickly now, he said: "If these lads of yours dare lay a hand, Lord, you'll be making your own bed for a while! And pay no mind to my large friend's rude and thoughtless blustering. He likes to haggle a bit, you see. But in any case, we accept the task you've given us. Without reservation."

"We *what?*" howled Eldin, turning his head to stare wide-eyed into Hero's suddenly placid face.

"We'll do it," insisted the younger man, but the look on his face—that look which Eldin knew of old—said much more. It said, "Be still, old friend, and we'll be all right. Do as you're told and we'll come out of it laughing . . ."

"Well," said Kuranes, breaking into the unspoken conversation without ever knowing it was going on. "Does your friend go a-questing on his own, Eldin the Wanderer, or do you go with him? Think carefully now, for I'll not ask you again. What's it to be: Zura, or Leewas Nith's dungeons?"

For a while the tableau remained frozen, then Eldin sank back into his chair. "Lord King," he said, his voice a low growl, "—is it possible these buckoes of yours could bring us another bottle of wine?"

A Hasty Departure

Later, Captain Limnar Dass found the pair digs in the city and stayed with them well into the night. They went out on the town with the captain, drank and joked with him, enjoyed his company as they rarely enjoyed anyone's other than their own—but were nevertheless glad when he left them at last and they were able to return to their lodgings. Finally, as they prepared for bed in the attic bedroom of an old tavern on Serannian's outskirts, Eldin was able to ask the one question which had been burning him up since their audience with Kuranes.

"Right," he began, "now what's all this about me not being the only thief in dreamland, eh? Was that your way of saying that—"

Hero, placing his finger on his lips, silenced him. "Even walls can have ears," he cautioned. He dug into the pocket of his jacket where he had folded it onto a chair beside his bed, produced a ruby which was the twin of the one Eldin had stolen, tossed it across the room. His burly companion caught it in cupped hands.

"How in hell—?" said Eldin.

"Easy," Hero whispered. "One minute after I took it

I had a premonition. A sense of impending nasty. I popped it into Limnar's pocket in the Museum and took it back from him when we were safely away from the place. If the Curator had stopped me, I was clean. If he had stopped Limnar—well, I didn't think that likely. As it happened, he stopped you." He grinned. "If he's since carried out an inventory . . . I guess he'll be going rusty with a rage right now!"

"He's not the only one," Eldin's chin began to jut. "If I remember right you gave me a pretty hard time after I was caught. And you blacker than the ace of spades!"

"That was to allay Limnar's suspicions, dolt!" Hero's grin broadened. "We couldn't have him mistrusting both of us, now could we?"

But Eldin was no longer listening. Instead he held the gem up to the glow of a lantern. "Oh, look at it, look at it!" he breathed in ecstasy. "It must be the most beautiful stone I've ever seen—next to the one I gave back."

"And as you said," Hero reminded him, "we'll live like kings for five long years on this one stone alone."

"One stone alone," repeated Eldin. Then his frown reappeared and he was suddenly gloomy. "Huh!" he snorted. "*If* we survive this damned quest, that is! And believe me, survival is no easy thing in Zura."

Hero shook his head sadly. "You really are getting old, my friend," he said. "Be certain we're not going questing for Kuranes or anyone else. Not to Zura. Not while we're rich as a couple of lords. Oh, we'll go along with him for now, by all means—but only for now. Then, as soon as we're off Serannian, at our very first opportunity—"

"We weigh anchor and shove off, right?" said Eldin, gleefully.

"Right," Hero emphatically agreed. "Now let's get some shuteye, yes? Tomorrow is another day."

* * *

Hero dreamed dreams within dreams of all that had passed since his arrival with Eldin in Serannian. Over and over his sleeping mind repeated—with certain of those inexplicable variations which dreams invariably insert into the order of things—Kuranes' explanation of the threat against Serannian, against the entire dreamlands. It had started three years ago with a visit, when two alleged Priests of Zura had arrived in Serannian as passengers on a galley out of Celephais. Gray-robed the two had been, their cowled faces gray, unsmiling shadows.

Because they said they hailed from Zura (and said it in voices which were flat and gray as their robes and shadowy faces), people tended to give them a wide berth. Also, there had been an odor about them, a certain smell which not even the most powerful perfumes could mask. It was that fetor which old sailors remembered from days when their ships had plied all the seas of dream, when they had inadvertently sailed too close to the shores of Zura.

For in those days Zura had been known as the Land of Pleasures Unattained, because the beauties and wonders its shores displayed had never been able to disguise the reek of plague-stricken towns and the soul-wrenching stench of gaping cemeteries—which was that same charnel odor surrounding the so-called Priests of Zura. Still and all, while the inhabitants of these saner regions of Earth's dreams felt uncomfortable about Zura, too little was known of that mysterious land to warrant any sort of action against its people; certainly not against its "priests." Thus that gray-clad pair came and went without hindrance, and when they went took their odors with them. Their odors . . . and something else.

For their interest while in Serannian had centered chiefly (though covertly) in the mighty engines beneath the city, in them and in the ethereal stuff they manufactured. And so great had that interest been that one of Serannian's less scrupulous engineers had been persuaded to obtain for them several small bottles of the stuff undiluted by the air around Serannian, in combination with which it formed the Cerenerian Sea.

The Priests of Zura were soon forgotten, however, and the city in the sky went on as of old. Nothing had changed (or so it appeared at first sight) and no one had suffered from the incursion of the gray-robed men from a forbidden land. Then, almost three years after those evilly odorous priests took their departure . . .

A man of Serannian, a sailor, was found adrift on the Southern Sea off Oriab, lashed to the shattered planking of some wrecked vessel, more dead than alive and babbling a fantastic tale. As luck would have it a merchantman returning to Celephais fished him from the sea, and one or two aboard knew him for a crewman on *Cloud Treader*, one of Kuranes' warships. Indeed the shattered fragment of hull which alone held him up from green deeps bore that very legend in flaking green paint: *Cloud Treader*, out of Serannian.

Some days later, shortly after the merchantman put into Celephais, Dyrill Sim (for that was the sailor's name) recovered his senses and was able to tell something of the wrecking of Kuranes' man-o'-war. What he told of the sinking of *Cloud Treader* was sufficient to warrant his passage on the next ship out of Celephais bound for Serannian, with a bevy of physicians by his bed to carefully tend his needs and return him to full health. And in Serannian he was taken straight to

Kuranes, who listened to his story with growing apprehension.

Cloud Treader had been one of Kuranes' fleet of warships, unused since the Bad Days but kept in good repair and sent out upon occasional missions and maneuvers into the skies of the dreamlands. Unlike the rest of dreamland's ships, Kurane's sky fleet was not dependent upon the buoyancy of the Cerenerian Sea. No, for in their holds the warships carried such quantities of ethereal aerial essence that each was a self-sufficient unit capable of sailing dreamland's skies away and beyond the limits of the Cerenerian. Moreover, should there be any leakage of that essentially non-existent stuff, then each ship had its own small engine with which to manufacture more.

How then, Kuranes had asked Dyrill Sim, might a ship such as *Cloud Treader* fall out of the sky and plummet like a stone into the Southern Sea, there to founder and sink, and all her crew with her with the sole exception of Sim himself? The survivor had answered thus:

One beautiful day—on a cloudless morning when the freshly-risen sun was bright and warm and the gulls wheeled and cried about *Cloud Treader* where she sailed high over the Southern Sea—with the Isle of Oriab lying far below and to starboard, then the lookout had spied in his glass an unknown vessel under full sail coming toward them out of the sun. *Cloud Treader*'s captain had thought that perhaps she was another of Kuranes' vessels—indeed, what else could she possibly be?—and so had come about and lowered most of his sail to allow the stranger to come within hailing distance.

Because she sailed out of the sun, however, the newcomer's lines were indistinct and her flag unreadable.

Then, when she was close and the golden orb of the sun no longer blinded, the men of the man-o'-war saw that this was no vessel out of Serannian but a ship of Death!

Her sails were leprous gray and her hull and Kraken-carved figurehead were dull, lifeless black. Only the eyes in the carven octopus which served as a figurehead had any color at all, and they were of a baleful red. The flag she flew was the skull and crossbones, and lining her decks the crew was formed of silent, gray-robed, hooded figures whose half-hidden faces gazed emotionless and yet with dire intent upon the *Cloud Treader* where she rode, all unprepared, upon that ocean of the upper air.

Then, feeling a terror within himself and waves of fear rising in his crew, the man-o'-war's captain had ordered full sail—but too late. Even as *Cloud Treader* began to draw away from the pirate, so her strange black cannons opened fire. Fist-sized cannon balls struck *Cloud Treader*'s hull and crashed through, and one shattered as it flew through the gunwales and onto the deck. It was filled with a gushing green vapor which quickly dispersed. No poison this, for those who saw and smelled it were neither offended nor made ill. If not an agency immediately inimical to life, then what?

But now, amazingly, the man-o'-war began to list to starboard, tilting toward the pirate. Now too her gunners had recovered themselves sufficiently to aim their ray-projectors at the decks of the black ship and the leaden figures of her crew where they stood at the rail. Brilliant beams of light raked those decks, passed over the massed, unsmiling crew of the grim vessel—with no visible effect whatever! Those deadly beams, effective against all manner of evil and nightmarish life in the dreamlands, were utterly impotent where the black pirate and her crew were concerned.

And at last the meaning of the green vapor became clear. For as more cannon balls entered *Cloud Treader*'s hull, so the man-o'-war tilted further yet, and it was seen that the vapor must be a nullifying agent which destroyed the power of the ship to stay afloat on the air. While *Cloud Treader* wallowed and her crew uselessly blazed away with their ray-projectors, so the pirate circled around and began to pound her port side. And now it was plain that the man-o'-war was doomed.

Down below, something broke in the engine which made *Cloud Treader*'s flotation essence. The engineer, working frantically to restore life to the precious device, knew that he was fighting a losing battle. Slowly but surely the man-o'-war was sinking, drifting down through deeps of the sky, falling toward the surface of the Southern Sea far below. And the pirate fell with her, circling, firing her cannons; until the last, as the final dregs of *Cloud Treader*'s life-essence were dispersed, she gave up all pretence of buoyancy and fell like a meteor from the sky.

Dyrill Sim remembered little of that mad rush to the bosom of the deep green Southern Sea, except that he had been aloft and in the rigging and that when a sail ripped loose and fluttered free, he had flown with it. Then he remembered the wash of the sea, and how he had lashed himself to shattered planking, and a mad, half-conscious vision of the black ship sailing down out of the sky to alight upon slowly swelling waters.

Now a voluptuous female figure rode astride the evil octopus figurehead, shouting commands as her crew of silent, gray-clad—zombies?—swarmed over the sundered wreckage of *Cloud Treader*, seeking something out. And finally, before darkness overcame him, Dyrill Sim saw *Cloud Treader*'s essence-engine ripped loose and held up to the beautiful yet strangely enigmatic woman where she sat astride the Kraken figurehead. She laughed with a voice that tinkled like bells and said:

"Let the sea take it! It failed the so-called 'man-o'-war,' didn't it? Well, then our engines are better. Zura's engines are better, and with her engines and her cannons she will become queen of all the dreamlands. Princess of Death and Disaster I am already, and soon I shall extend my charnel gardens through all the lands of Earth's dreams. Did you see Kuranes' ship fall? Aye, and how much more wonderful *his entire sky-floating city*!"

And these terrible words that fell so naturally from the strange woman's lips, and her wicked laughter tinkling over the Southern Sea, were the last sounds Dyrill Sim heard before falling back unconscious upon his raft of shattered timbers . . .

Hero awoke with a start and grabbed at the massive fist which bunched around his nightshirt and roughly shook him. Eldin, already dressed, grinned down at him and said: "Wake up, lad, for a new day's a-dawning. Limnar Dass is downstairs waiting for us, and I can smell breakfast hot in a pan."

"Dass? Here?" Hero mumbled. "What the hell for? Has he fallen in love with you or something? Is that what's made you so happy?"

"We're rich, aren't we?" Eldin replied. "We should be rich *and* miserable? Is that what you want? Anyway, Dass has been chosen as captain of the vessel Kuranes promised us. He's really pleased about it. Him and his entire crew, at our disposal. Aye, and the good ship *Skymaster* too."

All omens and miseries and memories of bad dreams fell quickly away from Hero as he dressed. Then the two descended from their garret room into the tavern proper and breakfasted with Dass. While they ate the captain told them that *Skymaster* and her crew were waiting, all provisioned and ready to set sail, and in less than half an hour they were riding the Tilt down to the sea wall and Serannian's harbor.

As they parked their bicycles and made for *Skymaster*'s gangplank, a sudden commotion in the crowding sailors and sightseers who thronged the wharf side some distance away attracted their attention. Something striding, metallic, purposeful, was coming toward them. Eldin took one look at Hero's suddenly frightened face and yelled:

"All aboard who's going aboard! C'mon, Dass, let's move it. Make way, there! Make way for the cap'n.' And he dragged both Dass and the strangely dazed Hero through the crowd and up the gangplank. Once aboard, without pause, while Dass looked on in utter astonishment, Hero shook off his peculiar paralysis and he and Eldin directed that the gangplank be raised at once and the ship steered away from the quay.

Finally, in a tone which bordered on the hysterical, the captain demanded: "What the hell do you think you're doing? You've got us all aboard, fair enough, but *I'm* the captain of this ship. We sail when *I* say we sail!"

"And are we ready to sail?" asked Hero breathlessly, his anxious eyes staring at the wharf where the colorful crowds melted to let through a metal, vaguely anthropomorphic being.

"Yes," answered Dass, "we're ready."

"And do you really want to go a-questing with us for the sake of the King and for Serennian?"

"You know I do."

Before Hero could say another word, Eldin roared: *"Then get this bloody hulk away from the quayside!"*

Now Dass spotted the Curator making straight for *Skymaster* as she pulled slowly clear of the quay, and the look of blank amazement on his face slowly turned to one of boiling anger. "Why, you—" he began.

"Later," said Hero, his face regaining a little of its color as the gap widened between quayside and ship. "For now—please tell your crew to make haste!"

Dass swallowed hard, then shouted out a few tense commands. The ship's scarlet sails billowed and she rode out onto the ocean of air. Now the Curator stood on the quayside, his arms extended to their full—which fell short of *Skymaster*'s dangling ropes by a good yard. Dass looked down at him briefly, then turned to Hero. "Give it to me," he commanded. "Give it to me now, or damn you—I'll take her in again!"

"Come now," Hero began, at which the captain put his hands to his mouth and made as if to bellow more orders. "All right!" Hero shouted. "Here, take the damned thing!" And he handed Dass the great ruby. Dass looked at it once, turned and threw it straight at the Curator. With a movement so fast that it defied the human eye, the metal man snatched the ruby from mid-air. He gazed at the stone with his crystal eyes, then switched that gaze to Hero and Eldin where they stood together at the rail. His eyes turned a glowing scarlet and one off this metal arms slowly came up to point out and away, far over the sea.

"The end of a beautiful friendship," grunted Eldin. And to the Curator he shouted: "Don't worry, old clanker, we're going,"

"He's not only telling you to go," said Dass with grim finality. "He's warning you never to come back. Not ever!"

Sky-Pirates of Zura

The plot was to have been that *Skymaster* would sail close to Zura, put off the adventurers at some advantageous point inland, and that they would then proceed as best they could on foot, employing their natural talents to get into Zura's heartland and there obtain samples of the green vapor. As King Kuranes had had it, the trick would then be to get out again.

As plans go it was a simple one. Simple things are often easy, and the easiest way is often the best ... On this occasion, however ...

On the third day out of Serannian, toward evening, as they passed high over Oriab and headed for the distant coastline of the Southern Sea, gray sails were spied in the southeast. Dass knew well enough that this could only be a pirate; this was not the Cerenerian Sea and therefore no other ship (except one of Kuranes' own fleet, of which none but *Skymaster* was in the vicinity) could possibly sail the skies of this region.

Northwest of *Skymaster*'s position lay a thick cloud-bank. Dass turned the prow of his vessel for cover and raced toward the clouds. Alas, Zura's pirate fleet was growing! Out of the clouds sailed two more black ships to block the man-o'-war's escape, their cannons firing even as they came—and one of them had a Kraken figurehead whose crimson eyes burned like malignant fires.

"Aye, well, we've cannon of our own, now!" cried Dass. "Which we didn't have before Zura sank *Cloud Treader*." He shook his fist at the enemy. "More conventional cannon than yours, true, but damned destructive for all that. Get the ports open, lads," he roared. "Let's give these dogs a taste of their own medicine!"

Still cleaving for the dense cloudbank, *Skymaster*'s cannons roared and rattled, and the stink of powder and hot metal came reeking up to Dass, Hero and Eldin on the bridge. And whether by sheer good fortune or expert gunnery made little difference, but no sooner had *Skymaster* loosed her first fusillade than two of the masts of the closest pirate crashed down, taking the third mast with them. In another moment the ship turned broadside to *Skymaster*, whose second barrage literally cleared the decks. The crippled black ship drifted away, silent and ghostly, and disappeared into the clouds.

Meanwhile the Kraken-prowed pirate had not been idle. Her cannons had poured shots into *Skymaster*'s flank, balls which issued green vapor within her hull's flotation chambers. Already the man-o'-war was listing badly to port, and behind her the first-sighted pirate rapidly gained on her. A fool could have seen that she would never make the cloudbank. Dass was no fool; neither were Hero and Eldin fools.

"We're done for!" cried Hero in impotent rage. "*Skymaster* will go the same way as *Cloud Treader*: down into the drink! Damn their black, piratical hearts!"

"Never mind the histrionics," snarled Eldin. "And anyway, it's not quite the same, is it? *Cloud Treader* didn't matter a damn to us, but *Skymaster* does. Hell's teeth, we're on board her!"

Now, because she was listing to port, *Skymaster*'s gunners couldn't get the necessary elevation to hit the Kraken-prowed vessel. Instead she blazed away at the third ship, just coming into range of her starboard cannons. The pirate flagship, seeing *Skymaster*'s plight, drew closer and pulled alongside.

"They're going to board us!" shouted Hero. "Now that's something we can handle. Eldin, quick, up into the rigging." He scrambled aloft with Eldin close behind him. Limnar Dass caught on fast and followed them, shouting down to his crew and pikemen to make ready their hand-weapons.

Now, with their hulls almost touching, *Skymaster* and the pirate slid by one another. As they passed so the vast majority of the gray-cowled pirate crew leapt aboard the crippled ship, swords at the ready. This was exactly what Hero had anticipated, and as the pirates left their ship he swung aboard her. Eldin and Dass followed suit, dropping lithe as cats onto the black decks of the enemy.

In another moment the two ships had separated, stranding the three aboard the pirate. Since the crew of that black vessel was now greatly reduced, however, they found themselves in a far healthier fix than the men left behind on *Skymaster*. At least they had a deal more room in which to make their play.

Hero wasted neither time nor opportunity but leapt at the closest pirate and sliced his cowl-hidden head clean from his body. Down went the man without a sound— without even a crimson spurt of blood—and another sprang to take his place. This one Hero stabbed in the heart, his sword passing through him as if he were made of cheese . . . except that when he dragged the blade free the man failed to fall but kept right on fighting! Out of instinct and desperation Hero struck again, and this time his blade tore aside the pirate's hood. Beneath it—

—A fleshless skull leered with empty sockets and rotting teeth!

And now Hero knew where he had smelled that fetor before—that reek which made vile the very air aboard the black ship—that stink of death and of those who should have lain themselves down long ago! However inarticulately, Eldin's howl of horror told how he had made the same discovery, while Limnar's *hiss* and gasp spoke for him. The three of them were fighting corpses, dead men who felt nothing of their blows and came on secure in the knowledge that they could not die twice!

Indeed, judging by the utter recklessness of their attack, it seemed that they must long for death, or at least an end to this monstrous undeath. Back to back the three men stood, forming a triangle as their rotting assailants crowded in on them.

"Go for their heads," cried Eldin, his voice a hoarse, nightmare croak. "If you cut off their heads, they fall!"

"Same goes for their legs," yelled Dass. "They keep on fighting, but they're not so nimble!" Even as he yelled his sword stuck in the skull of one leaping corpse and was dragged from his hand. Throwing himself forward in a frantic attempt to regain the weapon, he tripped over a headless heap of bones and tattered sinews and fell sprawling. Instantly the stinking crush pressed forward, trampling him down and circling Hero and Eldin with a band of flashing steel. Then—

"Take them alive!" came a laughing, tinkling female voice from close at hand. "Alive, do you hear? Let's have some fun aboard *The Cadaver*. We too seldom have living guests to entertain. To entertain *us*, that is!"

And again there came the tinkling laugh.

Now if words such as these had issued from a burly, bearded, peg-legged brute in a tricorn hat, and if they had been framed in a deep, coarse, bellicose voice, then they should not have been out of place. As it happened, when Hero and Eldin disbelievingly turned their heads in the voice's direction, the shock of what they saw was so great that they almost dropped their swords.

"Enter the pirate chief," whispered Hero in awe. "And what a chief!"

"If that's a pirate," said Eldin with a gulp, "it's me for the bounding main!"

The brief lull in the fighting was all Zura's corpse-pirates had needed. Two of them, coming on Hero and Eldin from behind, pinioned their arms so that others could step forward and wrest their swords from them. Dass was dragged unconscious to his feet and lashed to the mainmast, as were the two adventurers. Only then did the pirate vessel's mistress come forward, and only then was her astonishing beauty fully revealed.

Tall and leggy, she was clothed in a single fantastic garment which covered her arms, back, belly and thighs but left the rest of her body quite naked. Golden sandals accentuated the scarlet paint of her toenails and tight, wide golden bands on her wrists drew one's eyes to her slender, tapering, perfectly formed hands . . . but only for a moment. The rest of this Princess of Zura was likewise perfectly formed, and no man's eyes—lest they be already sightless—could possibly resist its beauty.

And yet it was a tainted beauty for all that. An almost visible aura of evil seemed to surround her, and outward from her washed waves of near-tangible terror. Her huge, black, slanting eyes that shone and missed nothing, seemed imbued with the hypnotic gaze of a serpent; and serpentlike, too, were the ropes of shining black hair which fell about her shoulders.

Her lips were full and red—too full, perhaps, too red—and they parted as she breathed to permit the flash of teeth like twin bars of white light. A thin film of heavily perfumed oil covered her body, giving her breasts a milky sheen where they stood proud and high and tipped with dark-brown buds.

And now, as she paraded before her captives, hands on hips and surveying them first over one softly rounded shoulder, then the other, so Eldin whispered: "Man, she's *edible!* And I know which bits I'd eat first!"

"Not likely you'll get the chance," Hero growled back. "And anyway, I'd employ a food-taster, first, if I were you. Edible? Carnivorous, more like. Why, just look at that mouth! That lovely maw of hers could suck out a man's very soul!"

It seemed that Zura might have heard him, or at least divined his thoughts, for she stepped closer and as her gaze swept Hero up and down it slowly turned from one of proud insolence to open admiration. "Men of the waking world," she finally said, and she cast a cursory sideways glance at Eldin. "Both of you—but you've come a long way from your origins. A pair of rebels who can't seem to find a place to settle in the dreamlands. Am I right?"

Hero nodded. "Near as damn," he said. "And what of you? What do you do with this brotherhood of corpses?"

"Do with them?" she laughed and threw back her ropes of hair. "I rule over them! For I am Zura, Princess of the Charnel Gardens and soon to be Queen of all Nightmares. As for these," and she swept her hand to indicate the ranks of undead, "these are my minions, the zombie denizens of Zura, the Land of Pleasures Unattained."

Her eyes returned to Hero and narrowed seductively. She licked her lips and reached out a slim hand in which a razor-honed, curved dagger was lightly clasped. Deliberately she sliced upward from his navel, and the buttons of his jacket and shirt went flying to the black boards of the deck.

Now she put away the dagger and stroked the adventurer's broad chest, her huge eyes widening again at the strong pounding of his heart and the pulse which showed its steady beat in his throat. Then she stepped back from him. "Cut this one loose," she said to her cowled, silently crowding crew, "and bring him to the rail. Let him see the fate of them that defy Zura. Then . . ." and again she licked her lips, "then we shall see what we shall see."

Zura's Tale

Leading Hero to the rail, Zura said, "There, see what becomes of my enemies!" She laughed and pointed out across the sky to where Kuranes' crippled vessel foundered and shook and trembled as shot after shot battered it to a hulk. The corpse-pirates—those of them who survived—were off *Skymaster*'s deck now and aboard the other black ship, and it was that ship which kept up the devastating bombardment.

Even as Hero watched through narrowed, flinching eyes, the man-o'-war's decks were raked with a broadside. Her masts and rigging were carried away at a stroke and green vapor writhed over everything. Gaping holes in the vessel's hull issued clouds of the stuff, and its effect on *Skymaster* was obvious and terminal beyond any doubt. As the last of her flotation chambers were ruptured, so she rolled over and slid down out of the sky, leaving rapidly dispersing green smudges to mark her trail. Hero could not tell if anyone remained alive on the doomed ship, but certainly none would live through the fall.

Zura laughed again and leaned far out over the rail to watch *skymaster*'s dreadful descent. No master of the sky now, that once proud ship, but a tumbling plank, a rag of sailcloth and a whistle of air through tattered, fluttering rigging.

"Thus perish all my enemies," said Zura triumphantly.

"Your enemies?" growled Hero with a half-sneer. "It was you attacked us, remember?" For a single moment he considered tipping her overboard and only the fact that they were under the silent scrutiny of a horde of sword-wielding zombies stayed his hand. "And was *Cloud Treader* your enemy too?"

No sooner were the words out than he could have bitten off his tongue, for Zura at once straightened up and turned to him. Her eyes widened as she leaned forward. "Ah! You know of that, do you? And what else do you know, I wonder?"

"Er," he answered, thinking quickly, and added quite inanely, "bad news travels fast in the dreamlands."

"Were there survivors, then?" Zura frowned. "That was careless of me . . ." And her eyes narrowed to the merest slits. "But if Kuranes knows it was Zura sank his ship, why has he sent out another to its doom? Or was she on some special mission, perhaps? Where was the man-o'-war bound, my brave young man of the waking world?"

Again Hero wracked his brains for an answer. "She was bound . . . for Ilek-Vad!" he finally answered, and held his breath.

"Possibly," Zura said at last, "since Kuranes counts Randolph Carter as one of his greatest friends. Would they cement a pact against me then? It would avail them naught."

"I know nothing of any pact," said Hero. "My colleagues and I were visiting friends in Serannian. The captain of *Skymaster*—now gone down with his ship, poor man—was an acquaintance. Since he was under orders from Kuranes to sail for Ilek-Vad, and since that city was our destination also—"

"He let you sail with him, eh? Well—what's your name?"

"Hero," he answered. "David Hero." And he hoped it was a name she had never heard of.

Apparently she never had. "Well, David Hero, you may never see Ilek-Vad. You may never see beyond the deck of this ship! Do you know that?"

He nodded. "I'm neither blind nor daft."

"Just so," and she gave a sharp nod of her head. "Nor am I—and I do as I will with my prisoners!"

"Then do with me as you will," he said, and somehow managed to keep the beat of his heart steady.

Her serpent's gaze seemed to probe his soul and for long moments she was silent. Then she said: "You are either very brave or very foolish. Perhaps both. Certainly you are different, as are all men from the waking world. It was clever of you to come aboard *The Cadaver* that way. If you'd stayed aboard *Skymaster* you'd now be dead."

"Perhaps I'd be better dead," said Hero under his breath.

"Eh?" said Zura suspiciously. "Do you mock me?"

"I said, certainly I'd be dead," Hero lied.

Again her eyes became the merest slits. "Indeed you would . . . But know this, David Hero: alive or dead, either way you would still be mine. The only difference is that dead you'd obey my commands more readily; though fortunately for you, much more woodenly. You'll understand my meaning—soon."

She turned from the rail and waved her moldering "men" aside. Without another word she made for her cabin and Hero, who had no desire to stay where he was, surrounded by stinking corpses, quickly followed her. On her heels he breathlessly asked: "What of my friends? Eldin the Wanderer and Limnar Dass?"

"They are safe for now," she answered, opening the black, gold-inlaid door of her cabin and beckoning him inside. As he moved to pass her she arched her body against him and said, "Be sure you do nothing to change that."

Briefly, as light flooded in through the open door, Hero saw a richly furnished, low-beamed room whose fittings were of gold and whose drapes were of a black, funereal velvet. Then Zura closed the door and it was as if they stood in gold-flecked blackness.

"Come, David Hero, sit with me and talk. Since you are coming from Serannian, you must know a great deal of that sky-floating city. Perhaps you know things which I do not."

"I think," he answered, sitting on the edge of the bed where she now indolently sprawled, "that I should rather know about you. After all, I'm a mere commoner—a man late of the waking world, yes, but a commoner for all that—while you . . . why, you're a princess!"

"A princess, yes," she answered moodily in the gloom of the place. "Princess Zura of Zura—Mistress of Death!"

"But from what I've seen of you," he pressed, "that's the way you like it."

"I have lived with it, grown with it, reveled in it!" she answered. "I would have it no other way. Listen and I will explain . . ." As she spoke she got down from the bed and sat at Hero's feet where she began to loosen his boots. Her movements were languid but sure and Hero made no move to stop her. Indeed he felt half drunk with her sensuality but his ears were wide open and receptive to her every word.

"When the dreamlands were young a certain wandering sorcerer fell in love with a girl who died before he could make his love known. Her death, though accidental, was horrible: she drowned in the Southern Sea off the shores of Zura—at least where the land of Zura now lies—and her body washed ashore there. Using his sorcerous powers, the bitter magician returned her to life; that is to say, he made her one of the undead, a zombie. Then for a little while he could talk to her, and she to him; but while his love burned like a fire hers was born of slavery and could never be real. There is no love in death, you see, and she could only say to him those words he bade her say."

Now Zura kneeled on the bed beside Hero, slowly peeling off his jacket. As she did so, she continued with her story. "In a little while, however, the sorcerer's dead love could no longer repeat even the few words he demanded of her. The human tongue is soft and does not last long after death. Still the sorcerer would not relax his hold over his love, and where he went she followed—until she no longer could. Then, blind to her loathsomeness, he stayed with her; and their tent stood in that place where now stand the Charnel Gardens . . .

"At last the morning came when, rising up from his blind madness of remorse and anguish, the sorcerer saw his love as she really was. He saw the worms crawling in her and the bones sticking through in places; and when he commanded her to open her eyes, then he saw the pus that seeped from peeling eyeballs. And tearing at his hair, at last he commanded that she be still; and so she sank down and melted into corruption . . ."

Zura paused a while to push Hero's shirt back from his shoulders and slide its sleeves down his arms. She kissed his neck and ran trembling fingers over his powerful shoulders. Hero, every fiber of his body burning, fought to keep his hands still and his heart quiet; but it was a losing battle. The blood was rising in him and Zura's perfume was in his nostrils. Her nearness and her silken hands worked on him like powerful magnets on iron filings.

Suddenly stifled, he stirred himself up a little and stared about at a room grown more visible as his eyes became accustomed to its dim light. The small, round windows were of red glass which added a ruby shade to the infernally wicked look of the place, and Zura's bedsheets were of black silk. Now she was stroking his hair, pushing him back until he lay stretched out.

"Go on with your story," he gulped, his nostrils detecting something other than the heavy reek of perfume as Zura's tongue flickered over her lips and she breathed close to his face. She drew back, paused, pouted, then continued:

"When the sorcerer saw what was become of his love—and more especially when he discovered that his body, too, was now diseased, infected by her rottenness—his madness returned tenfold. And this was the weird he worked in his great madness:

"That henceforth Zura would be the final dwelling place of all in the dreamlands who die fearful deaths. That such undead would hasten to Zura, there to serve their evil mistress, also named Zura, who would be the only living being in that entire land of death. Moreover, his weird was greater than this: for the sorcerer knew that a living princess must surely die if she were constantly surrounded only by legions of the undead. And so his curse contained this clause:

"That while Zura's princess must love the dead, she

might on occasion *renew* her strength by battening upon the love of the living!"

"And he used sorcery to ensure that his weird would come to pass?" gasped Hero in Zura's embrace, his head swimming with the closeness of the place.

"Aye," she answered, "great, mad sorcery!"

"And the name of his love," cried Hero as he sat up. "Of the one who was drowned in the Southern Sea. What was it?"

"Have you not guessed?" she answered, her fingers at his belt.

"Zura!" he shuddered. "And now you, who bear her name, would renew yourself with me!" Head reeling, he jumped from the bed. And so overcome was he by opiate fumes, and so weak from the lusts which had neardestroyed him, Hero almost fell. Instead, stumbling about, he collided with Zura where she had risen to her feet in a rage. His hand caught at her single garment and tore it down—

And despite the dimness of that room, now Hero recognized the source of the repellent musk whose queasy reek he had detected above that of poppy-essence and the scents of hideous, hybrid orchids; and he knew why Zura's dress had been designed to cover only certain regions of her body. For these were the sites of contamination—and he had almost become a sacrifice to her revitalization, her "renewal"!

Zura's upper arms bore the deep, black indentations of corpse fingers, and the heart of her womanhood was puffy and leprous with decay. Great raised blotches obscured what should have been the perfect outlines of her thighs and belly!

Staggering away from her, Hero snatched up his jacket and threw it over his shoulders. He tripped on something and sat down with a thump on the richly carpeted floor, and finding his boots he automatically began to pull them on. And one mad question rang over and over in his brain like a peal of crazed bells, until at last he found it bursting from his tongue.

"Zura—damned bitch of hell—what did your last lover die of?"

"My last lover?" she answered with a shriek of hideous laughter. "What did he die of? So you are blind after all, David Hero. Fool, he was *already* dead!"

Zura's Delight

With Zura's mad laughter ringing in his ears, Hero stumbled to his feet and found the cabin door. As he lifted the latch and threw the door wide, Zura opened a large, hitherto unnoticed cupboard set flush with the wall at the head of her bed.

"My lover?" the demon princess screamed again. "Would you really like to know him, David Hero? Then know him!" And out from the dark recess of her cupboard stepped forward a tall, nightmare apparition whose jerky, creaking movements and moldering aspect froze the adventurer solid where he stood framed in Zura's doorway. The thing had a short, wide-bladed sword in its claw of a hand, and as Zura pointed at Hero and screamed a command, so it lurched forward.

Galvanized into action, Hero ducked under the zombie's arc of steel and caught at the stringy wrist which controlled the sword. A moment more and he had wrested the weapon free—the entire hand, too!—and with a single sweep decapitated the cadaver which had been Zura's "lover." Collapsing, the body of the poor thing fell against him and threw spindly arms about his neck. With a cry of horror and loathing Hero tried to

disengage himself, only to be surrounded in a moment
by the rest of ship's graveyard crew. No longer having
room to move, still he surged and bounded in their
midst as they took away his sword and heaped themselves upon him. He found himself forced to his knees,
saw the bright gleam of a blade where bony hand lifted
it above his head, and—

"Hold!" came Zura's command, her voice ringing
loud and clear over the creak of leathery joints and the
clacking of bones. "No, no, lads, don't kill him. Not
that way, at least. I want him to come to me as a corpse,
but he can't come without his head, now can he? So
let's play a little game with our guests instead, should
we? That most *delightful* of all games." Her voice became a dangerous purr: "Poor David, did my perfumes
make your head spin? Well, what better way to clear a
dizzy head than a short walk in the sweet, clear air,
eh?"

She laughed and made to chuck Hero under his chin
where he was held in tight restraint, but he jerked back
his head with a growl of disgust. Zura's eyes hardened
and her lips curled into a sneer. She turned swiftly and
pointed to the ship's rail. "Get out the plank!" she
snapped her orders to the zombie crew. "There's no
shorter, sweeter walk in all the dreamlands than that!"

While Hero was roped back into position alongside
his colleagues at the base of the mainmast, a narrow
plank was dragged into view and made fast to the deck
so that one end projected far out over the abyss of air.
Limnar Dass had regained consciousness by now and
his eyes were taking in all of the activity at the ship's
rail. To Hero he said:

"This game she plans for us. Do you know it, my
friend?"

"I've heard of it," Hero gloomily answered. "A so-called 'sport' of olden-day pirates in the waking world. This must be Zura's version. But better by far than some of the games she likes to play."

Eldin snorted his disgust. "When I saw her drag you away into her cabin there, I said to myself, 'well, that's us in the clear. She'll be so taken with him that we'll all three be set free.' Huh! I might have known you'd let me down again. It would be a different story if she'd chosen me."

"Would it?" said Hero. "Let me tell you, old lad, you'd be far better off with a leper in the final stages of disintegration. Our little Zura there is a mobile cesspit!"

"Hero," answered Eldin. "let's not fool each other now, not in what promises to be our final hour. Truth to tell, I'd rather *live* in a damn cesspit than walk that plank!"

"No, you wouldn't," Hero shook his head.

"Damn me, I know my own mind!" snarled the other. "Don't tell me what I would or—"

"Why don't you two shut up!" hissed Dass. "If you must fight, save it until they cut us free of this mast. Personally, if I'm to die I'll take as many of these zombies with me as I can."

"The crew doesn't mean a thing without Zura," Hero informed. "She's the threat. If you've got to die a martyr—certainly if you want to save Serannian—Zura's the one to kill.

"What did you find out?" Dass urgently questioned. "Quickly, for one of us might yet escape to carry a message back to Kuranes. Have you discovered why Zura wishes to destroy Serannian?"

Both Hero and Eldin looked at Dass in amazement. "Escape?" said Eldin. "Limnar, you never fail to astound me. Sometimes I think you're daft as Hero! How in hell can we possibly escape?"

"Damn it, I don't know," Dass answered, "but if—just *if*—one of us does live through this . . ."

"All right," said Hero, "listen and I'll tell you what I think. Zura the woman told me that anyone in the dreamlands who dies a horrible death ends up in Zura the land, as a zombie in her Charnel Gardens. In other words, all her subjects are dead. Well now, during the Bad Days there must have been a fairly regular flow of unhappily defunct folk into Zura, but since then things have been pretty quiet . . ."

"So?" Eldin pressed, interested despite himself.

"Corpses," Hero informed, "rot! Zura the woman needs a regular source of supply. The fall of Serannian out of the sky would mean a massive injection of life—excuse me, death—into her Charnel Gardens. I think that that was the initial idea, but since then it's expanded. Gone to her head. Now she wants to be Queen of Nightmares, mistress of all she surveys. And where the dreamlands are concerned, she wants to survey all!"

"She wants to murder everyone in the land of Earth's dreams?" Dass gasped.

"That's the way I read it, yet," Hero nodded. "And it looks like we're to be among her first victims. Here she comes now!"

"Him," said Zura, striding up close and pointing at Eldin. "The ungainly one. See how the ropes chafe him? Poor creature. Him we shall set free from his misery at once . . . From all misery!"

"Ah, Zura, you've come to your senses at last!" cried Eldin. "Hero would be no good to a woman like you. He's only a pup in my employ. Come now, set me free and we'll—"

"Silence!" she snapped, and to her crew: "Fetch the dog!"

Kicking and struggling and roaring like a wounded

bull, Eldin was cut loose and dragged across the deck, then prodded with sword-points until he swayed out onto the narrow plank. A wind had come up and *The Cadaver* was rolling a little, so that Eldin shuffled and danced to keep his balance as he was prodded to the plank's outer extreme. To get him into position, Zura's zombie crew used long, sharply pointed poles.

Hero had gone chalk white against the black mast. Straining his neck to watch Eldin's performance, his muscles never ceased from bunching and cording as he put every effort into bursting free; but all in vain. Dass, too, was distressed almost to tears. "One at a time," he kept saying over and over. "One at a time, and we don't stand a chance. And poor Eldin, he's first to go. One at a time, Hero, one at a time . . ."

"Oh, for my sword," roared Eldin as he wavered and teetered at the end of the plank. "Is this any way for a man to go? With empty hand? A man who's been a fighter all his dream-life?"

Hearing him, Zura nodded to one of her crew and Eldin's straight sword was produced. She took it, weighed it for a second, gave it into the crumbling hand of a great black Pargan who threw it, without delay, toward Eldin. At that exact moment the ship gave a great heave to starboard as a sidewind caught at her sails. Eldin, thrown off balance, nevertheless reached for the sword and snatched it from the air. That was the end of it. He cast one last despairing glance in the direction of Hero and Dass. For a second only his eyes met Hero's—then he was gone.

"*Damn and blast your foul black heart, Zura!*" Hero howled, anguish choking off his words on her name. He gasped a while longer, gulping at the air. Then brokenly, more quietly, he continued. "Throw me down next, Zura. Me . . ."

"As you wish," she nodded, ropes of black hair blowing in the wind. She came closer and stood on tiptoe to stare into Hero's eyes. "But first . . . a parting kiss?" She licked her lips and held her face up to him.

The agony slowly went out of Hero's eyes. He smiled a strange smile and bent his face down to her—and spat at her point blank. She fell back, wiped the thick spittle from her wrathful brow and pointed a trembling hand toward the plank. "Go, then, fool!" she hissed. "But we shall meet again, you and I, never fear. In the Charnel Gardens . . ."

Hero was cut free from the mast and without delay was bundled onto the plank. He too was given his sword, and at the last he turned to face his tormentors like a great wolf at bay. Crouching there, inches from eternity, his eyes found Zura's and bored into them. For a second she met his ferocious gaze, then could meet it no longer. And when next she looked Hero too was gone.

That left only Limnar Dass, and without a murmur, head held high, he followed his friends of so few days along the plank and out into the sea of air. Zura watched his tumbling, rapidly shrinking figure until it entered clouds where they had gathered below like foam of ether. Only then did she turn from the rail.

A picture of Hero's face, furious, full of hatred and loathing, burned in her mind's eye. She felt a chill wind on her like some strange omen.

"Set sail for Zura," she ordered. Then, lifting her voice: "For Zura, I said, and quickly! That's enough sport for one day . . ."

Enter Gytherik

Eldin and Hero knew only one way to fall: noisily! But you can only yell for so long. They had yelled, both of them lustily, but more out of defiance of the unacceptable than in fear. You may fear death's approach when he is stealthy and his shadow falls over you slowly until it shuts out life's light, but when he leaps on you suddenly with his scythe already swinging ... Now they merely fell, tumbling, breathlessly, between whirling heaven and earth, expelled by the one and attracted—fatally—by the other.

Limnar Dass, on the other hand, knew a different way to fall. If the pair who preceded him rapidly down leagues of sky and had his experience of the air-baths, they too might have made the same desperate attempt. An attempt not to fall but rather—to fly. For in the air-baths Limnar had learned the best way to hold his body in order to maintain a position without sinking to the end of his chain, and if it worked in the air-baths perhaps it would work here. Not so efficiently, no, for while in the air-baths perhaps it was simply a matter of maintaining one's balance, here the fight was against gravity, a most powerful adversary.

In the waking world Limnar would have made a re-markable free-fall parachutist, but he had never lived in the waking world. Here in the dreamlands he could only do his best, and that without any parachute at all. Nevertheless, during those first few moments after casting himself from the plank, he had formed his body into the air-enclosing posture of the free-faller, and from this position he could observe through eyes half-closed against the whipping rush of his fall all that went on below.

In this position, too, he shot through the cloud-layer far beneath *The Cadaver*; and only then did his speed become apparent, so that he knew for sure that try as he might he could in no way slow his fall. The only difference, if he could maintain his present spread-eagled position, would be that he would be conscious when he hit the surface of the Southern Sea. Or at least, until immediately *before* he hit it . . .

And down below he spotted the hurtling figures of his two friends—Eldin plummeting like a stone while Hero seemed to pin-wheel down the sky—and a sick feeling of defeat came over Limnar as he realized that he would see the two hurtle into the sea, and that a few moments later he would follow them. From this height it would be like falling onto solid rock.

Then—

An impossible sight! Limnar slitted his eyes more yet against the rush of air and stared at the speck which was Eldin. He must be close to the surface of the sea by now, mere seconds away. And yet another speck—a winged speck—no, *two* winged specks, seemed to be converging upon him. And even as Limnar watched through streaming, disbelieving eyes, so the three merged together . . .

To Eldin the nightmare seemed unending, and yet as he saw the dark ocean looming larger with each revolution of his ungainly body, so he knew that indeed it was drawing to a close. And he was even more astonished than the watching Limnar Dass when suddenly he spied, falling with him into the deepening dusk and closing with him by the second, a great pair of gaunts whose faceless heads seemed angled to monitor every slightest change of position in his tumbling body.

Their bat-wings were folded back so that they fell like arrows, and it flashed through Eldin's mind that they might be scavengers racing to drag his shattered, exploded remains from the reddened wave crests. But gaunts, having no faces, are equally void of appetites—at least they have none that are mentionable. Certainly not for that sort of fare, anyway.

Eldin still held his sword clenched tightly in his hand, and for a moment he considered whether or not to make his final act in the dreamlands one of destruction. Yet he could not bring himself to strike. Astoundingly, he somehow felt that the gaunts meant him no harm— not right now, at any rate—and that his sword was holding them at bay from . . . what? If they meant him no harm, then perhaps they were trying to help him. Was that possible? But they wouldn't help him a damn as long as he flashed his sword at them! And quickly, fighting the rush of air, he sheathed his blade.

The effect upon the gaunts was immediate, electrifying, and life-saving. They angled their folded-back wings, swooped in upon Eldin, caught at him with their prehensile paws and dragged him through a straining downward curve which, as it flattened out, ran so close to the surface of the sea that he thought he could taste the salt spray.

Then the curve began to climb once more as the gaunts bore him up higher; and higher still he could see in the darkening sky the silhouette of two more pairs of flyers with human figures suspended between them. No, there were *three* other groups in the sky, and as Eldin strained his eyes to make out the shape of the third, so he gasped his amazement.

For the third was the silhouette of that great gaunt he had seen once before, and sure enough it bore upon its back the dark blot of a rider!

Now, straining to hold their human burdens aloft, the gaunts wheeled and made for the looming landmass of Oriab, and in the space of a minute or so they were flying close enough together for Eldin to shout across to his equally bewildered companions: "Hey, you two! Are you all right?"

"Aye," yelled Hero in answer, and:

"Aye," came Limnar's reply.

The parties closed with each other until soon only the great gaunt and its lone rider were left outside of hailing distance; and now Hero gave voice to his thoughts. "Eldin, what in thunder is all this about?" he demanded. "The last time we saw this performing aerial troupe they were trying to tip us out of the sky—trying to kill us. Now they're saving our lives! What do you make of it?"

"The only one who can answer that question for you," Eldin shouted back, "is riding that great gaunt there. And listen, we might have been at odds with him last time we met, but right now I'm all for him."

"Do you know the one who controls the gaunts?" questioned Limnar Dass. "But this is fantastic! If ever I get back to Serannian, they'll never believe me. Gaunts? Saving the lives of men? Why, it's unheard of!"

Now they were winging over Oriab and the lights of the island's great port, Baharna, were beginning to gleam as the sun sank down below the western horizon.

Without pause the gaunts sped on, and now the three found themselves growing increasingly uneasy as night deepened. They shouted questions to one another, even a little banter, but for all their assumed levity each knew that his voice was pitched too high, and so they quickly fell into silence. Soon only the throb of membranous wings and the chill whip of the air remained to fill in the night's darkness.

Then in the distance the three spied mountains and finally great jagged crests of rock where they stood as black silhouettes against a sky full of stars. "Those are the mountains of Oriab," Eldin informed his companions, and more quietly: "And I've heard some damned strange things about 'em, too . . ."

Now the gaunts began to circle lower until they alighted upon the narrow rim of what looked like the cone of some small, prehistoric volcano. Depositing their human cargo upon the rim, they again took to the air and flapped wearily away. A moment later there came the throb of even greater wings and the largest gaunt of all landed on the far side of the rim, its rider firmly seated upon its hunched shoulders. The moon now rode the night sky and silvered the newcomer's face, which was young, not especially cruel, indeed . . . a little frightened?

For long moments the gaunt-master and the group of three exchanged searching glances. Then—

"Well, lad," said Eldin in a fatherly manner, beginning to make his way carefully around the precipitous rim toward the spot where the great gaunt perched, "it seems we owe you our—"

"Stay where you are!" came a sharp warning. "You owe me nothing, and I owe you less than that. One step closer and I'll order my gaunts back and have you hurled from the rim. You may as well know it right now; I'm sworn to kill you! One wrong move . . . and your deaths will come that much more swiftly."

"You intend to kill us?" said Hero. "Then what the hell are you playing at? You could have let us fall into the Southern Sea—which would have done the job admirably!"

"After my first attempt upon your lives," the gaunt-master explained, "I decided that if chance permitted I would first tell you *why* I am sworn to kill you. Now I have that chance and so, before you die—"

"Cold-blooded son of a slut!" Limnar suddenly snapped. "I don't know what these two have done to you, but I for one have done nothing."

The youth on the gaunt's back inclined his head toward Limnar and pointed a trembling hand at him. "I have no quarrel with you," he informed, "but see that you don't anger me. Are these your friends?" And he tossed his head to indicate Hero and Eldin.

"Deny us," Hero urgently whispered. "If you'd save your skin, Limnar, deny us right now."

"They are my friends, yes," answered Limnar, ignoring Hero's advice. "Though I've known them only a little while, I believe that they're good men—basically. What can they have done that you should want them dead?"

"They murdered my uncle," said the other immediately, though without a trace of passion.

Hero looked at Limnar and shook his head in the moonlight. "We've murdered no one," he denied.

"Certainly no one's uncle," added Eldin.

"Oh, you do not know me," said the youth as he leaned forward to pat his gaunt's hideous head, "but I know you. My name is Gytherik Imniss, and my uncle was called Thinistor Udd!"

"Udd the wizard!" gasped Eldin. "So that's what all this is about."

"We killed a wizard in the Great Bleak Range of mountains," Hero quickly explained to Limnar. "It was self-defense. In fact, we didn't actually kill him. Aminza Anz killed him, but we had a hand in it . . ."

"I know that my uncle died by a girl's hand," said Gytherik, "and that she has gone where I can't follow her—back to the waking world. But you two were part of it, as you've admitted, and you are still here."

"Your uncle was a black-hearted wretch with evil designs on the entire dreamlands," Hero spat out the words. "When we put an end to him we did every man, woman and child in the dreamlands a great favor, including you, Gytherik."

"I know what sort of a wizard he was," answered the gaunt-master. "Aye, and that everything you say of him is true. Nevertheless I must kill you."

"But why?" asked Eldin. "If you had no love for your uncle, why do you seek to murder us?"

"Murder?" said the youth, for the first time uncertain.

"Murder, certainly!" cried Limnar. "If they killed your uncle out of duty to their fellow men, and if you yourself know that it is so . . . why, to kill them now would be nothing less than murder!"

After long moments Gytherik slowly shook his head. "No," he said, "it would be vengeance."

"But you didn't *like* your uncle," said Eldin, exasperation in his voice.

"Like him? I *hated* him!" cried Gytherik with feeling. "It's not *my* vengeance which falls upon you, Hero of Dreams and Eldin the Wanderer, but the vengeance of Thinistor himself!"

"But—" the pair began in unison, turning to each other, mouths agape in the moonlight.

"Now listen," Gytherik cut them short, "and I will tell you why I must kill you."

The Sorcerer's Apprentice

Slowly, carefully Gytherik dismounted to stand beside the great gaunt where it crouched on the far side of the rim like some monstrous gargoyle suddenly come to life. He stretched his legs for a second or two, never for a moment taking his eyes from the three friends where they faced him across the gaping throat of the dead volcano. The gaunt stretched too, shaking back its great bat-wings and craning its rubbery neck in a curious fashion.

"Yes," Gytherik finally began, "Thinistor Udd was my uncle—but no love between us, be sure of that. For where Mathur Imniss, my father, was good, his half-brother Thinistor was purest evil. They shared the same mother, you see, but their fathers were different. Thinistor was first-born, and his father was something of a sorcerer—a rather slipshod sorcerer, I gather—who vanished forever during some strange, necromantic experiment. It was almost as if he recognized the curse already sprung from his loins into the dreamlands, and that he deliberately removed himself as penance!

"Ten years passed and Grandmother took a second husband, my grandfather, Irik Imniss; and in Grandmother's last possible years, eventually Mathur was born. She died giving him life, and some nineteen years later, Grandfather followed her. Thinistor, the older half-brother, remained single, but when Mathur was in his thirties he met and married a young woman, my mother. By then my uncle was almost sixty years of age and he owned half of the house; Father owned the other half, living there with his new wife.

"Thinistor had inherited his father's appetite for sorcery, however—his books and apparatus, too—and as a result of the secretive and doubtful experiments he constantly carried out in his private rooms my mother soon came to loathe and fear him. As if to batten upon her fear, and despite the fact that he was her senior by forty years, Uncle Thinistor began paying her unwanted attentions; and this while she was carrying me!

"Now in all the years they had lived together, there had never been any love between the half-brothers. Mathur had worked and prospered while Thinistor studied the dark arts and frittered away his half of Grandfather's inheritance. Mathur had never liked Thinistor's experiments, but he was used to the other's strange ways and they had not greatly bothered him. Now, seeing that his wife went in fear of Thinistor and because she was carrying me, he reacted as any good man would. Since Thinistor was so much older, and thin and wasted by reason of his dark magics, the younger brother did not thrash him but merely threw him out; and he paid him more than fairly for his half of the house. Thinistor went, taking his books and other thaumaturgical devices with him.

"And the years passed . . .

"When I was old enough to understand these things my father explained them to me, and I have remembered. Thus, even before I knew my uncle, I hated him.

"When I was fifteen Thinistor came back and I met him for the first time. At first Father wasn't keen to see him again, but Thinistor held a trump card. He had been passing through Nir (where our house still stands) and had heard of my mother's sickness ... or so he said. Now, my mother's sickness was a strange thing, a sleeping, moaning, wasting thing, with which no ordinary physician could cope. For six long months she had suffered and declined, until Father was at his wits' end what to do about it. Then Thinistor came.

"He looked his age but was spritely enough, and indeed it seemed (or so my father told me) that he had changed. No more a mere wizard but a mystic, a man of great power—a traveling doctor who healed with his hands and his mind—Thinistor offered his advice, his services; and of course Father accepted.

"At first it seemed that all would be well. Mother responded wonderfully to Uncle Thinistor's treatment, which seemed to consist mainly of prayer, and she quickly returned to her previous strength and beauty. But as soon as she was well she turned from Thinistor. It was not that she was ungrateful, rather that her old fears had returned—and as it turned out, not without good reason.

"For although the old man had done nothing to arouse her suspicions, still she was obsessed by the idea that it was Thinistor she had to blame for her peculiar ailment in the first place. He had cursed her, she told my father, in order to 'cure' her and thus place us all in his debt.

"While my father laughed at her fears, his laughter was uneasy. For indeed he too was beginning to sense that Thinistor was not what he pretended to be. There was still that dark side to him, which day by day cast its shadow until the whole household seemed filled with its gloom. And still Thinistor had done nothing to deserve this covert condemnation—nothing which could be seen, that is. And obviously he was a good doctor (albeit a 'faith-healer,' as he had it) as witness my mother's complete recovery . . .

"It was then that my uncle began to take an interest in me. What he knew could be taught, he said, and he was thinking of taking an apprentice. He had a house in the Great Bleak Mountains, which was where he meditated, studied herbal medicines and worked to perfect his curative powers of mind over matter; all of which were important but subsidiary to his principal task, which was the cultivation of 'universal health and peace of mind.'

"Oh, yes—a very worthy man—my Uncle Thinistor . . .

"But no, my father would not hear of my apprenticeship to his half-brother, and so Thinistor must find himself another pupil. My uncle was displeased but said little. Father was in his debt and could not bring himself to ask him to leave; the very idea of throwing him out seemed unworthy, since through him my mother was returned to her full strength; and so Thinistor remained in his rooms as of old and returned to his studies. He would not stay long in Nir, he said, but must soon return to his own place in the mountains.

"Then, within the space of a single week, things began to change. My father's business, which was stoneworking and house-building, ran into trouble. He had planned and started to build five new cottages for families moving from Ulthar to Nir. Now they could not come, neither could they pay him for work already done. He had other jobs, however—repairs to walls and extensions to houses—and so turned to them; but within the space of a few days he fell and broke his arm. Then there was crop failure and prices rose alarmingly; and Father's arm was stiff and long in the healing; and people began to move from Nir to the shores of the Southern Sea where the fishing was good, and so things went from bad to worse. Night-gaunts were seen in the dusk over the hamlets of the plain, and people said this was the worst omen of all and made the old signs against great evil. It was as if a curse had fallen over Nir and the surrounding countryside, particularly over the house of Mathur Imniss.

"Again Thinistor broached the subject of my apprenticeship, offering Father enough gold to tide him through the bad times. And again Father denied him and told him to put the idea out of his mind. Then Thinistor grew angry and it was seen that indeed he had kept his real self hidden from our eyes. He left one night without saying goodbye, and we began to believe we had seen the last of him and things seemed so much better. Despite the fact that we were near penniless, at least we were happy again.

"So things stood for two long years. Then . . .

"One day my father took a walk alone in the hills as was his wont, but as dusk crept in Mother began to worry about him. He did not usually stay out so long. The lights of the town were coming on one by one as people lit the narg-oil lanterns in their houses and cottages, and still no sign of Father. In the end, to set Mother's mind at rest, I myself went out to follow the old paths he used, but searching was useless in the dark and so it would be better if I waited for morning's light. On my way home in the night I saw strange shadows in the sky which filled me with a great dread . . .

"We did not sleep that night, my mother and I, but in the dawn light went out into the hills to search for Father. We found the cane which he always carried, not really as an aid to walking but for its comfort and as a deterrent against hill-wolves or wandering zoogs, and also his pipe and pouch of herbs and thagweed—but of my father himself . . . Never a trace.

"Now the villagers knew and loved Mathur Imniss as one of their own. When they heard of our plight they came out by the score to help search the hills, woods, copses and ditches, all to no avail. They did find, close to where we had discovered Father's things, the footprints of huge gaunts in the sandy soil, but that was all. Father was gone, and news of his disappearance went quickly over the plain and into the neighboring towns. People began to lock their doors and windows at night, and to read omens in the dawns and sunsets and in the configuration of stars . . .

"I could get no work and Mother was sick with worrying over Father's unknown fate; our money had finally run out; the town's misers and moneylenders had their eyes on our large house and the walled plot in which it stood. In short, things were desperate. Mother began to talk of selling up and moving to a smaller house, but I wouldn't hear of it.

"Better times would come, I kept telling her. Father might yet return to us. Our fortunes were bound to change. If only I could find work, even a part-time job. If only this, if only that. If only we had accepted Thinistor's money and I had become his apprentice. It would have been for a few years only, after all . . .

"And as if he had been waiting for just such desperate times to come upon us—as if, indeed, he had plotted and planned the whole thing—that was when Thinistor returned. He said he had been in Ulthar where someone had told him of our troubles, and that then he had hurried to Nir in order to offer his assistance. And yes, his offer of work was still open to me. I was, after all, his nephew. Seeing our plight, how could he refuse to help us!

"Well, this was the opportunity I had prayed for, and my uncle's gold was as good as anyone else's ... And so I packed a few belongings, kissed my mother a fond farewell, and went with Thinistor back to the Great Bleak Range of mountains.

"You, David Hero and Eldin the Wanderer—you who killed Thinistor Udd—know well enough where he lived, and you also know that he was the blackest of all sorcerers. I too was made aware of the depths of his evil nature, but not until I had wandered through his cavern lair and found the monstrous black idol he worshiped there; not until I saw how the gaunts of night obeyed his commands; not until he himself told me how he had sent those gaunts to steal my father away from Mother and me!

"And I too might have killed him there and then, if I had been given the chance—except Thinistor made me a promise. That promise he made, it stayed my hand and made me his slave. And when he knew that he held me helpless, then he told me of his ambition to become the greatest sorcerer in all the dreamlands, commanding kings as they command common men. With the aid of what he had found in the great Keep of the First Ones, he was sure he would succeed.

"As for my poor father; he was safe and would remain so as long as I did as Thinistor bade me do; and indeed the wizard needed a helper. For as his studies and experiments had come to occupy so much of his time, there was precious little of it left over for the mundane necessities of life. More and more he had needed to make trips to the coastal cities for rare drugs, chemicals and olden books, which meant that he was left with less time for his damnable work. I, therefore, was to be not so much an apprentice as a messenger boy, a servant—for the moment. Later I would become more properly an assistant.

"In payment for my work, Thinistor had already given my mother a fair sum of gold. And I was to have my food, my keep, money in my pocket and a warm place to lay my head. Moreover, there was my uncle's promise, which was this: that providing I was obedient, patient and faithful, he would one day set free my father and let him return to my mother in Nir.

"And what would happen, I wanted to know, if Thinistor should fall victim (as had his father before him) to his own experiments? Who then would free my father from his unknown prison? In answer to which he worked the following weird upon me:

"That in the event of his demise by the inadvertent release of baleful spirits, or by any other malevolent power, then that I should learn the whereabouts of my father and set about his release as best I might. And should Thinistor die by any merely human act or agency, then that I should inherit all of his sorcerous knowledge, including knowledge of my father's where-abouts and the means to effect his release—*but only if I avenged my uncle's death and destroyed his killers!*"

As Gytherik paused to let his words sink in, Eldin took the opportunity to growl, "So if you were working for Thinistor, you must have known that he was holding an innocent girl up there in his caves?"

Gytherik shook his head. "No, I was away on his er-rands for well over a year before you killed him. In any case, he kept all such things secret, knowing that I could never be made to agree with them. It was only af-ter he was dead that I discovered his blackest iniqui-ties."

"*After* he was dead?" Hero sounded sceptical. "His ghost told you, then?"

"No, I saw it all in a shew-stone which he kept hidden in a secret place. The crystal recorded all that occurred in the caves and could be viewed over and over to the viewer's content. Thinistor said that it was something he had taken from the Keep of the First Ones. That is how I know that your Aminza Anz killed him— but only because of you two. Since she is no longer in the dreamlands, you alone may ensure the working of Thinistor's weird—by dying!"

"So what you're saying is that you yourself really had no part in these atrocities your uncle committed, eh?" asked Limnar.

"None at all."

"And yet you now intend to murder these two men in cold blood?" Limnar shook his head. "It doesn't add up."

During this exchange between Gytherik and Limnar, Hero and Eldin had been shuffling round the crater rim away from each other and toward the gaunt-master. Now they were halfway toward him, converging upon him where he stood beside the great gaunt. Seeing their less than stealthy approach, Gytherik climbed back into the small saddle at the base of his gaunt's neck. "Doesn't add up?" he answered Limnar. "Why not? Hero and Eldin mean nothing to me. I merely seek to rescue my father. I cannot do it while they live, and therefore must bring about their deaths."

Now, moving more quickly, the adventurers drew their swords and Hero cried: "You don't think we'll die easily, lad, do you?"

"Perhaps not," called Gytherik, "but still you *will* die!" He dug in his heels and the great gaunt bore him aloft, leaving Hero and Eldin facing each other in the wash of air from throbbing wings.

"You couldn't kill them!" cried Limnar. "It's not in you."

"No," yelled Gytherik from on high, "I couldn't, not personally. I suppose that makes me a coward. Well, what I myself cannot do, my gaunts can certainly accomplish for me. You—" he spoke to Limnar, "I've nothing against you. When the gaunts come, they shall not harm you—neither shall they help you. As you pointed out, this is murder and you are the one witness. Good luck to you—and farewell!"

The Caves of Night

They all three watched the great gaunt flap away into the night, Gytherik a black silhouette humped upon its shoulders, and then they turned to each other in a sort of controlled panic. Any normal sort of panic was unthinkable in their present predicament; the sides of the cone, inside and out, were sharp and sheer, and the mountains reached dark and unyielding down to the plain far below. The two adventurers threw themselves flat on the rim of the volcano and peered over the outer lip into sheer, unmitigated blackness.

"What are you doing?" Limnar questioned. "Surely you're not seeking a way down?"

"What else?" growled Eldin. "Would you like to help us, or are you here merely to observe and advise?"

"You just stay put, Limnar," said Hero, face down, his head far out over the abyss. "We've done this sort of thing before, me and Eldin. Climbing at night is not new to us." He paused. "But on the other hand . . . it's damned dark, and these mountains are totally unknown to us."

"Nor do we have a lot of time," growled Eldin from a similar position. "If only we had a good rope, then—"

"But we don't have," Limnar frustratedly cut in. Then, in rising excitement, he added: "We do have our clothes, though! My shirt is made of fine, strong, supple leather. What about yours, Eldin?"

"Mine too," answered Eldin, sitting up straight. "How about you, lad?"

"I . . . I don't have a shirt," Hero ruefully answered, opening his jacket to show a naked chest. "I think I left it in Zura's cabin."

Eldin snorted disgustedly but Limnar said: "Very well, if we tear these two shirts into strips—" and he pulled off his shirt and began to demonstrate. "See, we should be able to make ourselves a decent rope—albeit a short one."

Eldin needed no further urging but immediately followed suit. The moon was riding higher now, and by its silvery light they quickly knotted together some forty feet of leather strips, testing the knots as they tied them. When they were satisfied with their makeshift rope, Hero was given the task of choosing a place to lower it down the outside wall of the cone. This was sheer intuition on Hero's part, for in the moonlight every reflective surface of the near perpendicular face looked the same—yellow splotches on black velvet—but in the end he felt that he had made the best choice.

Then, tying one end of the rope to a knob of rock and tossing the other into space, he said: "Me first."

"No way," said Limnar. "I'm smallest and lightest by far—and I'm no mean climber in my own right. And don't worry, boys, for I'm not all afraid. You don't live all your life in Serannian without developing a head for heights, be sure. If there's a way down at the end of the rope, I'll find it. If not—" he shrugged. "Also, once I'm down so far, I'll be able to call directions up to you. Here we go—" And without allowing further argument he swung himself down over the sharp lip of the ledge and was gone from sight.

"Climbs like a monkey," grunted Hero in appreciation, stretching himself out flat on the ledge once more to watch Limnar shinning down the rope.

"Aye," growled Eldin, "so he does. You know, lad, I've grown to like Captain Dass. I mean, I really *like* him. If we were a trio instead of a duo—"

"You'd like him to sing tenor to your bass and my baritone, eh?" guessed Hero.

Eldin nodded. "He's a good man," he gruffly answered—at which juncture there came a twanging, snapping sound from below, then a short cry cut off by a dull thump, followed by the receding clatter of falling rocks, pebbles and loose shale.

"Or at least he was," Hero sighed.

The two peered over the rim into the abyss, a black emptiness shot with featureless gold, and slowly Hero pulled up the rope. He counted eighteen knots instead of twenty three. "Nearly reached the end of it," he said. "Damn me, Eldin, I feel rotten."

"Me too," said the other. "But let's face it, he wouldn't have stood a chance on his own. And in any case, we don't have the time right now for mourning. Listen—"

Hero listened, and sure enough he could hear the flap and throb of wings beating in the night. The sounds drew closer by the second, and there could be no doubting their source.

"Do you remember the way they hit our little boat?" asked Eldin as they climbed to their feet. "I reckon we're in bad trouble."

"Today," answered Hero, almost as if he hadn't heard, "I've been made to walk a plank two miles high over the Southern Sea, and I'm still alive! I don't intend to die now—not easily, anyway." And as he spoke a wild idea occurred to him. Eldin felt Hero's sudden tension and said:

"What is it, lad?"

"Listen," said Hero, "and do as I tell you. I think I know how we may yet come out of this."

He quickly outlined his plan, with Eldin nodding every now and then, and was just finished when the first black shadow came winging out of the night. The gaunt circled, was joined by a second, a third and a fourth. Eldin pointed at one with his sword. It was bigger than the others, with a thin body and vastly arching wings.

"Yes, that's the one, all right," Hero grimly agreed. "And because he's the biggest of the bunch, he might just be brave enough to attack first. In fact—"

"Here he comes now!" Eldin finished it for him.

Hero's plan was a simple one, but not a little dangerous. He intended that he and Eldin should use the largest of their attackers as a parachute. The danger lay in the fact that ordinary parachutes do not attempt to shake off their passengers, or otherwise deliberately do them harm . . .

Now the gaunt was almost upon them; but even as they ducked and prepared to fling themselves each upon a grasping paw, so the creature swerved and they saw its near-fatal subterfuge. From behind, skimming in low over the cone at the end of a whistling, flattening dive, one of the smaller gaunts seemed bent upon a kamikaze-style suicide. And indeed, if the adventurers' reactions had been but a fraction slower, they would surely have been swept to their deaths.

As it was they leapt away from each other, leaving a gap through which the small gaunt sped with mere inches to spare. And doubtless the rubbery creature would have lived to try again—had the pair been other than Eldin the Wanderer and Hero of Dreams. For as it shot between them over the extinct vent they simultaneously whipped up their swords and braced their arms—and wingless the gaunt went tumbling soundlessly into darkness, while a pair of fluttering membranous rags spun dizzily on the chill night wind.

And only then, while the two were off guard and caught up in the excitement of first blood, did the larger gaunt launch its true attack. In he came, faceless (and strangely furious for a gaunt), beating at the air with wings which would have flattened the adventurers if they had struck them. But quick as twin flashes Hero and Eldin grabbed at the gaunt's dangling, wildly thrashing limbs, wrapping their legs about its paws. Immediately the creature's wings began to beat faster as it took their weight, and for a moment it seemed that it might win against the greater pull of gravity. All was a blur of leathery body, vibrating bat wings and jerking, kicking limbs—until Eldin struck upward with his straight sword.

The idea was that wounded, the huge gaunt would flutter down to the plain to die. With luck the two would survive the landing and from then on they could fight on their own terms, undaunted by precipitous heights and the fear of falling from narrow, volcanic lava rims. Thus Eldin's stroke was not meant to kill but to wound, and then not too severely. Eldin had done the job for the simple reason that Hero's curved blade was too sharp—literally sharp as a razor—and he had judged his thrust just right. His timing, however, could not possibly have been worse.

For even the best laid plans are subject to the unpredictable, and nothing is less predictable than a nightgaunt. Neither one of the adventurers had reckoned on the wounded creature descending directly *into* the crater!

"Hell and damnation!" Eldin roared as the light was quickly shut out by the upward reaching sides of the vent. "Who's guiding the beast? I might have known that if *you* planned something, Hero, it would go all to cock!"

Hero, desperately trying to get a better hold on his chosen gaunt-limb, gasped: "I'll remember that, Mouth Almighty, when next we need some quick thinking done. Meanwhile, hang on for all you're worth—and whatever you do *don't* stab him again—*umph*!" And he sank his teeth into the rubbery, violently thrashing limb where it shook him like a pea in a whistle.

Their voices, mingled with the now erratic throb of wings and the amplified clatter of loosened debris from the walls, echoed and rolled in the confines of the vent. And so narrow that volcanic flue, and so dizzy their descent, that the adventurers were made to feel weightless, sick, and full of sensations of disaster as they plummeted in stygian blackness. The gaunt, incapacitated by its crushing cargo, by Eldin's thrust, and by the vent's claustrophobic confines, was hard pressed to do much more than fall, and for two or three minutes the two feared that indeed this was the end. If they struck bottom at this rate of descent, with the gaunt on top of them . . .

Then the great wings began to beat once more, however feebly, and after a while they arched into huge airtraps. The adventurers, where they clung to the gaunt's legs, felt their weight returning as the speed of their descent rapidly decreased and a cool but noxious breeze began to blow in their faces.

"He's gliding!" Hero coughed out the words. "How the hell can he see where he's going?"

"Just so long as he keeps on gliding, I'm not bothered," Eldin chokingly answered. "How do gaunts see anyway? No, right now I'm more interested in this night-black underworld."

"This great cavern, you mean?"

"This underworld," the Wanderer repeated. "These Caves of Night, as I've heard them called. Oh, I've heard tell of 'em, myths and legends and all—I know a little something about 'em—but I've never visited 'em. It's no place to visit, the underworld. Come to think of it, I don't know of anyone, except perhaps Randolph Carter, who *has* been here and lived to tell about it. I suppose there must have been some, though, else how did the tales get started in the first place? One thing's certain: this isn't a healthy place."

"Yes, well, I'd guessed that much," said Hero dryly. "For one thing it smells like a damned great tomb!" He eased his position a little on the gaunt's now limp leg. "Go on—what do you know about this . . . this underworld?"

"That it extends in burrows and caves and vast vaults under most of the dreamlands," Eldin replied. "Also, that in certain places it connects with the lands above. Oriab's mountains must be one such place."

"And there are others?"

"I've said so."

"Then we might possibly find a way out?"

"Possibly, if we could 'see' like our leathery chum here." Eldin waited for further questions and when none came added, "But we can't."

"Still," Hero eventually said, "if we survive our landing, and if—"

"If, if, if!" snarled Eldin. "Listen, lad, I hate to sound pessimistic, but surviving the landing could well be our biggest mistake! One: we'll be lost and good as blind.

Two: we'll very quickly exhaust ourselves groping about in the dark and bumping into things. And three: we'll soon become very hungry and thirsty. With luck we'll last a week—if we don't bump into any of the locals, that is."

"Locals?" Hero's voice was quieter. "You mean people live down here?"

"Who said anything about people?" Eldin answered and his voice carried a warning that Hero should ask no more . . .

The Snufflers in Darkness.

CHAPTER XV

As the gaunt grew weaker so its glide became faster and steeper; and as they plunged into the nighted bowels of the mountain the adventurers began to discern a faint luminosity to the foul air. Rushing currents of reeking mist carried a gray phosphorescence that swirled, adhered and silhouetted in glowing motes the gaunt's thin body.

The underworld was awesomely huge. High overhead, damp with glowing mist, an incredible ceiling of stalactites reached away into impossible distances; while below, needle-tipped spires marched in row upon endless row to indeterminate destinations.

"The Peaks of Throk," said Eldin breathlessly. "The infamous tips of mountains whose roots, it's said, go down to the pits at Earth's very core!"

Hero said nothing but gazed downward in growing alarm as the Peaks of Throk seemed to sweep upward, until the gaunt was threading a complex flight-path between them which left little more than inches to spare. The peaks were so sheer, smooth and regular that they were more like gray pillars which reached up immense and ageless on all sides. And so swift the gaunt's descent that soon the needle peaks were lost in dimly glowing heights, while below the pillars seemed to go down and down to black infinity.

Then, already dizzy with the endless blur of pillars as they flashed past and sick from the gaunt's nightmare rush and swoop, the adventurers closed their eyes against howling winds which sprang up sudden and unexpected; and when next they looked they found their view obscured by ash and yellow smoke, while their lungs contracted to the sting of brimstone-laden air.

But at last the winds blew themselves out, the smoke cleared, and finally the dread Peaks of Throk receded into obscure distances. Now the flight of the gaunt had leveled out, but its wings beat ever more erratically and the adventurers feared that each passing second might be the last.

And finally the head of the rubbery beast sagged upon its sinuous neck as, with a feeble swoop and a twitching of wings, the dying creature sought the unseen terrain below. In another moment Hero felt his feet dragging through pebbles and dust, and before he could relinquish his hold upon the gaunt's leg the stump of a stalagmite reared out of the darkness directly in his path.

With a blow that knocked that last ounce of wind right out of him, the stalagmite snatched Hero free of the gaunt's paw and tumbled him head over heels in dust and stony debris. Senses spinning and bones aching, he lay for long moments in darkness and strove to clear his head of wheeling stars. Apart from a sick roaring in his brain and the hoarse sound of his own breathing, all was silent now—too silent.

"Eldin?" Hero called, the sound of his voice seeming to whimper away like a whipped dog into the dark.

"Eldin, are you all right?" And then, more urgently, more desperately: "Eldin—speak up, man!"

Finally an outraged sputtering came from somewhere fairly close at hand. "Get this ... double-damned ... stinking heap of rubber ... *off my legs!* Hero, where in hell are you?"

"That's right!" Hero gulped his answer.

"Eh?"

"I'm in hell, or near as damn!"

"Get yourself over here," Eldin snarled. "Follow my voice. My legs are stuck under this filthy great carcass."

"Is he dead?"

"Well, if he isn't he's picked a funny place to go to sleep!"

"So what's the hurry?" Hero asked. "Surely we'll do well to save our strength, take things nice and slow and easy. I mean, there doesn't seem much point in rushing about down here." He made his way gropingly forward over stony, pebble-strewn ground until he found the gaunt's great body where it sprawled half on top of Eldin.

"Listen," said Eldin, grabbing Hero's arm, "just help me get free—and keep it quiet." The young man sensed his friend's fear, and Eldin afraid was an extremely rare thing.

"What is it?" Hero whispered, his scalp prickling. "What's troubling you?"

"I ... I thought I heard something," Eldin answered. "And in this place—if we're where I think we are— that's not good."

"Where you think we are?" said Hero. "But we know where we are, surely. We're in the underworld." He strained to ease the weight of rubbery flesh from his friend's legs.

"We're in a certain region of the underworld, yes,"

answered Eldin, dragging himself free. "The Vale of Pnoth, if I'm not mistaken."

"Pnoth?" Hero quietly shaped the word in his mind as well as with his mouth. He discovered that it left and unpleasant taste in both. "I believe I've heard of . . . Pnoth."

Eldin stopped rubbing at his cramped legs and again gripped the other's elbow, harder this time. "Look!" he hissed. "Did you see that?" And certainly Hero had seen or sensed something. A movement in the darkness—a peculiar, furtive humping of black shadows—a subtle alteration in the texture of the timeless night which surrounded them.

Or perhaps it was his imagination. For Eldin's remark about this place being the Vale of Pnoth had stirred both memory and imagination in Hero; and while the first was merely unpleasant, the second was positively frightening. He had remembered a fragment of information picked up somewhere long ago and almost forgotten; namely that the Vale of Pnoth was the home of strange and sinister dholes, though what a dhole was exactly he never had reason to inquire. He had heard, though, that they spent a considerable amount of time heaping bones; also that they neither greatly loved nor were beloved of men. Pnoth—dholes—imagination—

Nightmare!

Backing away from the body of the gaunt, their elbows touching and their hair prickling to its very roots, all sorts of monstrous notions rushed screaming through the minds of the adventurers. And as if to confirm Hero's worst suspicions, Eldin hoarsely whispered in his ear, "Dhole! . . . If he's scented us, we're done for."

"Scented us? Damn me, Eldin, even when you whisper you sound like an earthquake! Man, he'll *hear* us!"

"No," Eldin answered with an unseen shake of his

head, "dholes are deaf—I think. Never hear the expression 'deaf as a dhole'? Blind too—but they do have a wonderful sense of smell."

Still backing carefully away from the gaunt, swords in their hands and senses straining, suddenly the two were riveted to the spot by a sound which could only be likened to a noisy sort of snuffling; as if some vast bloodhound were slobbering and sniffing in the darkness. Then, as the sound stopped for a moment, there came in its place a sliding of pebbles—a brushing aside, as it were, of stony litter—and again the inky blackness seemed to stir and rustle and take on dim and frightful shapes.

The snuffling came again—closer, more decisive—and with it a return of mobility in the momentarily rigid limbs of the adventurers. More quickly now they backed away, careless of what might lie behind them; until, in another second, they stumbled, tripped and fell amidst a loosely piled heap of—

"Bones!" shuddered Hero, gingerly feeling of the ossuary fragments upon which he and Eldin lay.

"Pnoth!" Eldin nodded his affirmation in the dark. "I was right. And our unseen friend there—definitely a dhole."

Even as they lay there the snuffling and slithering continued, growing louder by the second, until Hero could stand it no longer. "The hell with this!" he cried, jumping to his feet. "Come on, let's get out of here."

"Wait," said Eldin, grabbing his arm. "Just a second. There's something I want to know. He should have just about found the gaunt's body by now ..."

"Oh, come *on!*" hissed Hero. "What can you possibly want to know about—"

"Shh!—Listen!—There, what do you make of ... of ..." Eldin's whisper trailed off, and listening to this new sound, Hero could well understand why.

The snuffling had increased to a sort of frenzied slobbering interspersed with sharp tearing sounds; and now, from afar and from all directions, there came a veritable chorus of minor grunts and snuffles of inquiry. Even as the pair listened, their ears straining to pick up every slightest nuance of the drama being enacted in the darkness, the tearing and slobbering abruptly stopped and was replaced by the loathsome sounds of bestial feeding; then this too ceased and there came a weird, mournful cry as of some strange nocturnal bird.

Answering, excited cries came echoing back, at which Eldin grabbed Hero's arm and said: "Now let's get out of here. The gaunt was a big one. Its carcass ought to keep them busy for quite some time." And Hero felt his friend shudder in the darkness.

As they slipped quietly away from that dreadful feasting place, they noticed that their eyes had become marginally accustomed to the dark. Not to any great degree, for the darkness of dreamland's underworld is black as any of the deepest caves of the waking world, but the surfaces of things seemed to carry minute traces of phosphorescence. Thus it was as if they moved across a terrain of black velvet streaked here and there with dim wisps of gray, and at regular intervals they would come across piles of bones whose individual shapes and hugeness set them—mercifully—aside from any possible human connection.

Direction gave them the greatest problem, for they simply could not be certain of their course, or even if they moved in a straight line at all. In a little while, however, the sounds of feasting died away behind them, and soon after that they came to the foot of a sheer cliff whose crags reached up into dimly luminous mists and vanished from sight.

For what seemed like hours then they followed the

undulating base of the cliff; and as they went so they talked in hushed, rather forlorn tones. Though they would never have admitted it, neither one of them had the slightest idea how this thing would work out, and both were aware of their growing hunger and thirst. It was only when they paused to rest for a few minutes and seated themselves upon black, unseen boulders that the monstrous morbidity of their situation seemed to settle over them like some clammy, ethereal cloak.

Then it was, too, that they discovered something of the persistence of dholes. For as they sat in silence so there came the first faint fumblings and rustlings from far back along their trail, and they knew that indeed the dholes had finished with the gaunt and now sought sweeter meat!

It was only with the greatest restraint that the pair held back from full-scale flight at that point. For even knowing that to panic would be to court disaster, still adrenalin filled their veins and power surged in their limbs; and near-irresistible urges bade them throw caution to the wind and flee . . . but flee where?

They did increase their pace, however, and for a while the sounds of pursuit grew fainter; but then— horror of horrors—secondary rustlings and snufflings began to reach them from their flank. Not only were there dholes behind them, but a second party was closing in from the plain of bones. Again they increased their pace and after half an hour or so reached a point where the cliffs turned sharply inward, as if this were some ancient subterranean coastline and they were entering a dried-out, prehistoric bay.

It was as they paused here at the corner of the cliffs and rested, desperately fighting to control their breathing and their tired, trembling limbs, that snuffling came yet again, and this time closer than ever. Moreover, the adventurers could no longer tell for certain just which direction the sounds came from. Still closer the dreadful night-noises came, and the pair remembered all too vividly the tearing and terrible gluttony which had accompanied the first dhole's discovery of the dead gaunt.

That memory was more than they could bear, and so they turned the corner of the cliff and sought safety in the bight of the rocky bay. With luck, they might even discover a slope they could climb to the top of the cliffs, and thus leave the dholes behind them in the Vale of Pnoth. Or if worse came to worst, perhaps they could find themselves some vantage point to defend to their last.

Now, because the death-fires were a little brighter here, the adventurers could see that indeed they had entered a great bay where in ages past the cliffs had fallen or been eroded away. The bed of the bay was littered with vast boulders and rocks, all of them dully aglow with that strange foxfire, so that it seemed to the pair that they ran across an alien moonscape. Behind them, echoing weirdly, they had started to hear the excited, nocturnal-bird sound of the hunting dholes, who must sense now that the chase was nearing its end. And when they dared to look back they could see great, undulating shapes across a wide arc of vision, humping and wriggling and forming a constantly changing horizon.

Then, rounding a massive boulder as large as a house, the two were brought up short at sight of something directly ahead. At the base of the cliffs where they loomed across some four hundred yards of comparatively debris-free plain, the mouth of a tiny cave emitted a beam of dim light which shone like a beacon to the tired and unbelieving eyes of the adventurers. There was a warmth to that dull glow, a reminder of lanthorns and campfires and other healthy lights in the upper world, and its lure drew the pair like moths to a flame.

Behind them and on both sides as they ran, the loathsome rustling, snuffling and hunting cries of the dholes rang louder by the second, and all of the darkness seemed alive with the unseen, unknown horrors as they closed in. Then the pair were pounding forward beneath the beetling cliffs, and the glowing cave mouth beckoned them on, and the shadows of the cliffs were alive with morbid movement, until with exhausted cries of gladness—yes, and of strange expectation too, for they knew not what they would find—they hurled themselves into the narrow mouth of the glowing cave and turned to face the terror which crowded upon them from outside.

Captive of the Cave

Beyond that peculiarly illumined hole in the subterranean cliff there might well have been a slow-burning lake of sulphur or some such combustible, and Hero and Eldin would have welcomed its fiery embrace rather than let their nameless pursuers, the snufflers in darkness, come upon them unseen. Even now, crouching in the tiny opening, they were less sensitive of what *might* be behind them than of what they *knew* lay outside. On entering they had received vague impressions of an extensive but low-ceilinged, gently glowing, stalactite-pillared cave, whose walls appeared festooned with luminous moss. They had seen nothing, however, to inspire fear in them—that is to say, more fear than already was present—and so their concentration was centered on the encroachment of the still unseen dholes.

In fact the dholes were to remain unseen, as they had always been and ever would be, though their humping shadows were plainly visible and their rustlings loud as they gathered beyond the cave's entrance. Gazing out along the dim beam of light from the cave's mouth, Hero felt prompted to whisper:

"Where are the damned things! I can see movement—

far too *much* movement—and I can hear them well enough, but I can't see a one! What's stopped them, d'you think?"

"The light," Eldin answered at once. "Things of darkness don't much care for light. Not that that helps us a lot. We've been given a reprieve, that's all. Have you had a look at this place?"

Hero turned from the cave's mouth and sheathed his sword. Together they stared all about them. And now Hero knew what Eldin had meant by saying that this was merely a reprieve. Because of the cave's luminosity, it was not hard to see that there was but one entrance. Which meant that they could only go out the way they had come in . . .

"Then we'll just have to sit it out," said Hero, shivering in a sudden chill. "Perhaps if we keep quiet they'll lose interest in us and go away. While we're waiting, I suggest we inspect our new quarters . . . *yeow!*"

Eldin jumped six inches off the ground at Hero's cry, his straight sword appearing in his hand as if by magic. "What?" he snarled, seeing nothing that might have caused Hero's howl of alarm. "What? What? Hero, you lunatic, you scared me out of five years' growth then! What happened?"

Hero was backing away from the wall, stumbling and almost falling with every backward pace he took. His sword, too, was back in his hand; with his free hand he pointed in a palsied fashion at the moss on the wall. Mouth agape, he seemed to find difficulty in articulating. "Moss—" he finally gulped. "It moved—the whole damn mass of it! It's alive! When I touched it—it moved."

Eldin, who had not suffered Hero's terrific shock, or at worst only part of it, stepped forward and lifted his sword to point it at the tangle of moss which Hero's outstretched hand indicated. He made as if to thrust, and—

"Kill me then, if you will!" cried the moss in a reedy voice, detaching itself from the wall and forming a glowing, manlike shape. "Kill me, you agents of Thinistor, and an end to your torturing ways. Ah! You don't fool me, for who else but wizard-spawn could come here, unharmed, across the Vale of Pnoth?"

Now, seeing that the gesticulating apparition was a human being draped in lightmoss—and a badly frightened human being at that—the adventurers held their swords a trifle less aggressively. Eldin addressed the trembling thing thus:

"Whoever you are, shake off that moss at once. I've a mind to run you through just for the shock you've given us. What's the idea of hiding there like that!"

"Who are you anyway?" asked Hero. "And what's all this about us being agents of Thinistor? Thinistor Udd, d'you mean?"

"Udd, yes, of course," answered the apparition, hastily shedding its glowing camouflage. "Since you know of him, he obviously sent you. Why keep up the pretense? As to who I am—you already know that."

Tall for one of dreamland's own and well into his middle years, the man was made to look older by reason of his flowing white hair, pallid complexion and almost skeleton thinness. His clothes, or rather their remnants, consisted of tattered ribbons of cloth that barely held together, and the index finger of his left hand—which he seemed to hold awkwardly—was shriveled, crooked, and white as if baked in a fire.

"Thinistor Udd didn't send us here," growled Eldin.

"In a way he did," Hero contradicted.

"*Aha!*" cried the stranger, cowering back.

"Oh, he sent us here, all right," Hero continued, speaking more to Eldin than to the other. "Or as good as. We certainly wouldn't be here if we hadn't killed the bastard, and if that young fool of a gaunt-master didn't need to kill *us* in order to find his—" And he paused. Eldin saw the understanding dawning on Hero's face and turned back to the ragged oldster.

"You?" he growled. "Is it possible that you—are—"

"I'm Mathur Imniss, which I'm sure you know well enow," answered the other. "And you'll never convince me that you weren't sent by that devilish half-brother of mine, Thinistor Udd."

"Listen," snarled Eldin, his patience on the point of evaporating. "For the last time, we haven't come down here to do Thinistor's work. Nobody ever will. He's dead, and we were partly responsible. We're here because of your son Gytherik—because he won't be able to find you and set you free until he's killed us . . ." Eldin paused, frowned, sheathed his sword. "It's complicated."

"My son?" Mathur came forward and clutched at Eldin's powerful forearms. "My boy? Gytherik sent you?"

"Er, not *exactly*," Hero said. "Look, let's all sit down and I'll explain right from square one. Before I do, though, I would like to be sure we're safe here." And he jabbed a thumb in the direction of the cave's entrance. "What about them?"

"Them?" Mathur Imniss repeated him. "The dholes?" He spat on the pebbly floor. "Cowards! Afraid of clean light. In fact, clean light would be fatal to them, I'm sure. They even fear this filthy stuff," and he held out a fistful of glowing moss. "Watch—"

Mathur moved quickly to the entrance and threw out the lightmoss, ensuring at the same time that his arm did not pass beyond the arch of the cave's mouth. There was an instant rustling and scraping as shadows which had seemed perfectly natural took on a furtive, fearsome (and now fearful) life. The darkness seemed to withdraw, and not only through the action of the dimly glowing heaplet of lightmoss where it lay beyond the entrance.

"Cowards," Mathur repeated. "Oh, you're safe enough here—but come, come, tell me all. What of Gytherik, and my good wife, his mother? And how is Thinistor dead? And if he is, how am I ever to be out of this place? And—"

"Whoa!" cried Hero. "Let me tell it on my own time." And without more ado, he did.

By the time he was done Mathur was reduced to tears. Not tears of self-pity—though that might have been expected even in a strong man—but tears of frustration. Frustration that his wife lived and loved him still and did not even know for sure that he still lived. Frustration that even though he was found at last, and by good men, still he was lost. Frustration that his son had been so close, physically, geographically, without ever knowing it. And the adventurers, feeling useless, could only watch until the tears dried up.

Finally Eldin said, "When we go, you go with us, Mathur Imniss."

Slowly the sad, ragged man shook his head. "No," he said, holding out his left hand to show them that shriveled, warped index finer. "No, for this is the nature of the spell which Thinistor laid upon me: that to step beyond the cave's mouth is to die, twisted, shriveled and blasted like this finger of mine. Once, when I was half-mad with loneliness and despair, I tested his spell. This zombie finger is the result. I held it out under the arch of the entrance for one second only. No, I stay here for the rest of my days—or until the spell is lifted.

"Or until your Gytherik does us in," said Eldin darkly.

"It doesn't have to be that way," Mathur said. "Thinistor always left counterspells to his spells. My spell—the one that holds me here—can be broken by breaking a shantak-bird's egg."

"But the shantaks nest beyond Inquanok," said Hero, "and they're notoriously fierce when it comes to protecting their eggs."

"Exactly," Mathur nodded bitterly. "Thinistor knew that, too. It was his way of extracting the last drop of juice from the meat of my predicament. How can I possible gain possession of a shantak's egg down here? For I myself must break the egg, you see, before I would be free to go. And even then I must find my own way out of here. An utterly impossible situation."

"Not if *we* could somehow get out of here—" Eldin began.

"—And somehow fetch you a shantak's egg," added Hero.

"Would you do that?" Mathur sprang to his feet, trembling with hope, hugging first Hero, then Eldin. "Would you? But how could I ask it of you? To go out from here, braving all the terrors of the underworld, and then to return! And in between, to journey beyond far Inquanok, there to steal the egg of a shantak-bird. No, too much—too much! No man could expect it."

"We're questers," said Eldin gruffly, overcome by Mathur's mixed emotions. "We—er, *enjoy* such adventures. Right, Hero?"

"Why, er, yes—right!" agreed the other. "Certainly we always seem to be getting mixed up in them. But you'd have to do your bit, Mathur. Perhaps you could start by telling us what you've learned of this place while you've been here? Maybe we could benefit from your experiences. You might even know a way out, forbidden to you through Thinistor's spell but passable to us?"

Mathur snapped his fingers with a sharp crack. "Perhaps I *can* help you! Well, not I myself, no, but—"

"But?" together they prompted him.

"My friend," he said.

"There's someone else down here?" Eldin looked sharply about. "I don't see him."

"He's not here right now," Mathur somewhat uncertainly explained. The adventurers frowned and looked at each other, and eventually Hero snorted:

"Not here? You mean he's out there—in the Vale of Pnoth?"

"Somewhere out there, yes," Mathur agreed. "You see, he's not human. In fact, I'm not even sure he's a he!"

Hero and Eldin sighed in unison and the latter asked: "I suppose you'd better explain. It's your turn, after all. What is this friend of yours? A gug, a ghast . . . a ghoul?"

"A ghoul!" exclaimed Hero, wrinkling his nose. "I really don't think we ought to have any truck with—"

"No, no, no!" cried Mathur. "He—*it*—isn't any of those. It's nothing I ever heard of before Thinistor put me down here. It's, well—it's a thing."

"A thing?" Hero and Eldin hollowly chorused.

"Yes," Mathur nodded. "A running thing."

The Running Thing

CHAPTER XVII

Suddenly, much to Hero's astonishment, Eldin cried, "Ben Gunn!"

"Eh?" said Hero. "Ben who?"

"Gunn, Gunn!" Eldin repeated, his irritation showing as he began to feel foolish. Dim memories from his previous life, momentarily glimpsed, were gradually receding. Of Mathur Imniss he inquired: "Do you, by any chance, like cheese?"

"My wife used to make it from goat's milk," Mathur replied. "Indeed I did like it—but why do you ask?"

"No craving?" questioned Eldin.

Mathur shook his head, bewildered.

"What's all this about?" asked Hero, frowning. "Cheese? Ben Gunn? Craving . . . ?"

"Forget it!" Eldin abruptly snapped. "It's just something I seem to remember from the waking world—I think. Not important."

"Well, good," said Hero. "Fine! And now that's done with, do you think we might lend ear to Mathur here? What he's trying to tell us might be *very* important!" He turned back to Mathur. "Would you like to continue?"

Mathur nodded and sat for a moment wringing his

thin hands. Finally he began. "There's not much to tell, really. Thinistor put his curse on me and had his gaunts bring me down here, to this very cave. He told me what would happen to me if I tried to flee the place—told me also that I could break the spell by breaking the egg of a shantak-bird—then left me here to fend for myself.

"During the first day—or for what I judged to be a day—I explored the cave. I found water dripped from stalactites into a pool back there, and some mushrooms. The mushrooms are different from those you find in the fields up above. They're fleshy, tough, not so tasty. But you can live on them. I have."

"You've lived on mushrooms?" Hero repeated him.

Mathur nodded once and continued: "Very sustaining, but not very fattening. Anyway, after I had been here some time—two days, three, a week, how can one tell?—then the running thing returned."

"Returned?" Hero queried.

"Oh, yes. This is where the running thing lives. It's his cave. I don't suppose Thinistor knew that. Or maybe he did—it makes little difference.

"As fortune would have it, I saw his return. I was sitting here close to the cave's entrance, just as we are now. I was gazing out into the darkness, still numb with the horror of being trapped down here. Then, out and away in the Vale of Pnoth, I saw a light. It was strange, that light, a glow like that of lightmoss—which as it happens it was—and growing larger and brighter, or so it seemed, by the minute.

"As it drew nearer so the unpleasant creatures of the vale grew silent, moved off, left it a clear path . . . which I was soon to discover led to my cave. Or rather, its cave. As I watched, frequently the light would disappear, obscured by boulders or heaps of bones; but always it grew larger, which warned of its bearer's rapid approach.

"Then it came—but not directly, not upon any sort of ordered or sensible seeming course. Just why he—it—runs that way I cannot say, but its mode of travel is strange to say the least. Here and there it moves, pausing briefly, then off again, as if searching—but for what? And then a sudden burst of speed for a hundred yards, and another pause, a dart here and a start there—and off again. But always closing with the cave.

"Soon it was plainly visible, moving rapidly across the clear area immediately in front of the cave; and as soon as I could make out its size and shape, then I became very afraid. I drew back and tried to hide myself, for suddenly it seemed to me that I might know the reason for the creature's crazy stopping and starting motion. Perhaps it was sniffing me out!

"Mercifully I was wrong, and still I don't know why the running thing does that. And something else: for all that he—I'm sorry, but I must call the creature 'he'—for all that he's different, I mean really different, still I envy him. He's not trapped in the cave, you see? At least he has the run of the vale—of all the underworld, for all that I know.

"Anyway, the other creatures of the underworld—the dholes and the rat-sized flea-things that infest them—they moved quickly away as the running thing came. Not only do they fear the lightmoss with which he lights his way, they also fear him. And with every reason! I have seen him ravage amongst them. And afterward the shadows they make are different. They don't move anymore; and the smell of their corpses lingers until the dark winds blow . . .

"And so he came to the cave. When he entered I was peeping out from between a pair of close-grown stalagmites; and though I believed myself well hidden, still he sensed me at once. With a start and a run and a great stiffening of his long fur—which made him seem three times greater in size—he found me and backed me up against the wall of the cave. His eyes examined me and his breath blew warm on my face. He opened his great mouth and his teeth were curved needles that grew in rows down the whole great length of his throat.

"I knew then that I was finished, that he was about to kill me, and so I fell to my knees before him and offered up prayers to the Great Gods of Eld. I had no weapon; what else could I do? Should I throw myself into his jaws and simply end it like that? No, prayer seemed to me to be the right thing, and I have always served the Gods of Eld. And certainly it was my prayers saved me.

"For my prayers, or the voice that uttered them—my *human* voice—seemed to fascinate the running thing. A dog will rush at you snarling, and when you talk to him he'll wag his tail and sniff your hand and whine . . . and eventually sit down at your feet to be patted on the head. So it was with him. As I prayed out loud so he gradually closed his great mouth and moved closer, listening, purring his pleasure. Ah, yes—it's a strange and moving sound that: when the running thing purrs.

"Well, as you probably know, the chanted prayers to the Elder Gods are a form of singing. And so it dawned on me that the running thing likes singing, that he would not attack me so long as I sang to him . . ."

"Hero sings," Eldin interrupted, hardly bothering to disguise his disgust. "He's a poet, too."

"Then he'll soon make friends with the running thing," said Mathur.

"Right now," Hero yawned, "I would much rather

make friends with a bed of this lightmoss. I never felt so knackered!"

"Me too," Eldin agreed, fighting to stifle a sympathetic yawn of his own.

"Of course you're tired," said Mathur solicitously. "You must be, after your flight across the Vale of Pnoth. Very well, I'll show you how to make your beds. We can talk again when you're rested. My own bed's on a ledge deeper inside the cave."

They bundled together twin heaps of moss and the adventurers stretched themselves out fully clothed. Mathur, because he was too excited to sleep, simply sat and watched them. Before closing his eyes, Hero thought to ask: "Mathur, just how d'you suppose the running thing can help us get out of here?"

"Why, he would carry you out, of course!" the oldster answered.

"Carry us?" Eldin rumbled, half asleep. "Both of us? Just how big is this running thing?"

"Oh, he's big," answered Mathur. "Indeed he is . . ."

Five times the adventurers slept, and they ate mushrooms until Eldin complained of them coming out of his head. Time seemed to stand still in the continual sameness of the place and the newcomers soon came to despair of the running thing's ever returning. Which was just about when the creature chose to return . . .

They were all three seated on large stones near the entrance when a faint will-o'-the-wisp light appeared out in the Vale of Pnoth. Hero saw it first but tended to believe that his eyes, dulled with monotony, must now be playing tricks with him. He blinked, rubbed at his eyes, stared harder out across the shadowy and menacing vale, and finally said: "No, I'm not seeing things at all. Or rather, I am. There's a light out there, a moving light!"

"Hmm?" said Eldin, lost in thought; and then, as Hero's statement took hold: "What? A light? Where?"

"There—" and Hero pointed.

"That's him," said Mathur, starting to his feet. "That's the running thing."

Now the adventurers grew apprehensive, and Eldin asked, "Just what measure of control do you have over this running thing, Mathur?"

"Control? I think he understands me, if that's what you mean. He does me no harm. I believe he enjoys my company."

"And you sing at him, right?" Eldin pressed.

Hero gave a nervous snort. "Hah! So you're beginning to wish you had a singing voice after all, eh, old lad? Perhaps you'll mock my tunes a little less in future."

"Look!" cried Mathur. "See—the way he stops and starts—to and fro and back and forth? Oh, that's the running thing, all right! When he draws nearer to the cave you'll be wise to get behind me. At least until I've introduced you."

"Hero," said Eldin in his softest voice. "I somehow know that I'm not going to like this. Look out there across the vale. See how the shadows seem to be drawing back? The dholes are clearing out. What sort of creature do dholes fear, eh? And Mathur says he's seen the running thing ravaging amongst them. Ravaging? Amongst dholes?"

The light was brighter now and rapidly approaching across the boulder-strewn ground some two to three hundred yards beyond the cave's mouth. No shape was discernible as yet, merely a dim-glowing aureole that zigzagged and darted and paused here and there like a wasp at a picnic. Then, with a rush and a scurry—with breathtaking rapidity—the thing shot across the final flat stretch of ground and came to an abrupt halt just beyond the cave's mouth. And as the dust settled about the thing's many, *many* feet, so the adventurers crept quietly behind Mathur and did their best to become very small.

"Hero," Eldin quietly croaked, giving his colleague a tiny dig in the ribs. "Do you know any good songs?"

Flattening itself to the ground, sniffing loudly like a bloodhound on someone's trail, the running thing entered the cave; and despite Eldin's horror—or perhaps because of it—a vague memory from the waking world of men stirred in his mind at sight of the thing.

"Oniscus Porcellion," he breathed. "Wood louse— but what a wood louse!"

The thing turned to them, its head swiveling, its many legs scurrying to swing its body around; and as if it took exception to Eldin's remark, so the mat of glossy hair on its segmented back rose up in an angry ruff. It sniffed at Mathur and nuzzled him as he hummed a greeting, then gently nudged him to one side with its plated snout. Now it loomed before the adventurers, its ruff stiffening, bright eyes glinting and great jaws partly open.

They could see the lightness which grew upon the thing's sides, forming a glowing oval all about it; they smelled the warm, not unpleasant odor of it—like the smell in the heart of a forest after rain—and they glimpsed its curving needle teeth as the jaws opened wider yet. It was then that Mathur said: "Sing, quickly, while he's undecided!"

From somewhere in his nose Hero forced an odd, trembling note. Then, drawing air, he began a tune; a trifle wobbly at first but gathering strength as he proceeded. It had no words, that melody, for it was an old cradle song, a tune to be hummed. The reaction of the running thing was immediate: it purred loudly and nuzzled Hero's chest. Then it lifted is head and turned its eyes upon Eldin.

Without pause the older adventurer cleared his throat. He put one hand on his chest, cast his eyes to the cave's shallow ceiling, opened his mouth—

And sang:

"Git arlong, liddle dawgee, git arlong—"

Escape from the Underworld

The trip through the underworld was fantastic for many reasons. Fantastic for the way in which it was achieved—upon the segmented, furry back of the running thing, which in motion felt like a cross between a rhumba and, especially on inclines, a roller coaster—fantastic also for the weird, otherworldly scenery it offered, and particularly fantastic for the speed with which it was accomplished.

As a prelude there had been three or four sleep periods, many hours of song, a lot of talking to the creature, even the unexpected spectacle of the running thing "ravaging" amongst a half-dozen dholes which encroached too close upon the confines of its cave, and finally its growing restlessness as it felt the pull of unknown wanderings in the labyrinthine underworld. And through every waking hour, over and over again, Mathur had talked to the creature, repeatedly explaining the requirement of the adventurers, that the great multipede convey them to a region from which they might make their way back to the world above.

And at last the pair had said their farewells to Mathur—making him their promise that they would not rest until he was free of Thinistor's spell and out of his prison—before climbing up onto the trembling back of the gigantic, music-loving, subterranean crustacean which their host had named the running thing. Then, with a breathtaking rush and a start they were off; and for all that they had known many previous adventures in the land of Earth's dreams, this was perhaps the strangest.

Hanging on grimly to the running thing's carapace where they lay upon its slightly curving, deep-fur covered back, the pair were not sorry when they cleared the Vale of Pnoth and entered a region of mighty stalactites. The underworld's ceiling was low here, mere hundreds of feet over their heads, and many of its great smooth stalactites met with stalagmites thrusting up from the floor to form tremendous columns.

Between these vast, natural supports, here and there, deep black pools of water made ebon mirrors of utterly glassy aspect. From one such pool, as the running thing darted by, a lashing tentacle erupted in a spray of inky water—but lashed in vain for the many-legged mount of the adventurers had already passed beyond its reach. This happened several times before the ceiling reared away out of sight once more and the pillars faded into the dim distances behind them.

Then they reached the shore of what appeared to be a great lake of pitch, onto the edge of which the running thing ran very briefly before returning at once to the sandy shore. There he scurried about in the sand until his many feet, covered with pitch, picked up a good deal of sand. The adventurers upon his back saw the reason for this peculiar seeming industry when, with a sudden rush that came close to unseating them, their weird mount shot out onto the surface of the lake and proceeded to run across it! With its feet encased in sandy boots, the creature had traction, and so marvelous its agility and so great its speed that its dusty feet were given no slightest opportunity to sink into the pitch.

As they crossed the lake Eldin remarked: "I do believe that this must be the Stickistuff Sea."

"Never heard of it," answered Hero, morbidly wondering what would happen if the running thing were suddenly to stop or trip.

"Of course you have," Eldin snorted. "Have you never dreamed that you ran in molasses, and however fast you ran you couldn't escape your nightmare pursuers? Myself, I remember many such dreams. Well, they all have their origin right here, in the black and horrible Stickistuff Sea."

"I believe you," said Hero in a very small voice, which caused Eldin to inquire:

"Eh? Something wrong, lad?"

"You could say that," Hero answered. "Don't look now but—you remember the nightmares that used to pursue you in those dreams of yours? Well, I do believe—"

But Eldin had already turned his head to look back.

And certainly this was the stuff of nightmares, for rising up in the lake behind them spidery, oily shapes sped in hot pursuit like black, alien skaters with eyes of glowing red. There were dozens of them, squelching up from the pitch like man-sized, six-legged skeletons that dripped oil even as they shot after the running thing in fiery-eyed hate and with fearful intent. And as these hideous pursuers gained on them, so the pair began to feel the now uneven beat of their mount's great heart and heard its ragged, sobbing breathing. Its feet sank ever deeper into the pitch and its speed slackened off by the second.

Then, putting on a burst of speed, the two closest

pursuers leapt for the running thing's rear and scrambled aboard. Hero and Eldin, swords glinting, met the lightning attack of the grinning pitch-things as only they could, sending twin heaps of lifeless, tangled sinew and bone flying into the path of the rest of the pack. This gave the running thing a brief respite, but in no time at all the pursuing horrors were right behind them once more.

Now, some two hundred yards ahead, they could make out a dim shore whose reflection formed a glassy image at the edge of the Stickistuff Sea. But more and more the running thing was tiring; its breathing came harsher and its sides heaved with exertion. The slapping sounds of its feet were individually audible as they moved more slowly yet, almost completely clogged with oil and pitch.

Again a pair of nightmare spiders leaped, and again they fell in tattered disorder. Then four more—all red eyes, black bones and yellow fangs—and the swords of the adventurers flickered like wands, glinting dully as they performed almost magically in the practiced hands of their masters.

Then, with a sickening lurch, the running thing skidded to a halt and toppled forward, its segmented body rising up like a whip to hurl the adventurers headlong . . . onto dry sand!

And now, in the shallow pitch at the lake's edge, the running thing turned upon its attackers in a fury, like a terrier at a rat pack. In a matter of seconds ten of the nightmare creatures lay in tatters while the rest fled in a rout, frenziedly skating back out into the Stickistuff Sea and sinking bubblingly from sight in black and glutinous depths.

In a very short while all was silence once more and the adventurers climbed to their feet and dusted themselves down. As for the running thing; he very soon recovered and proceeded to shake himself like some strange and gigantic hound, until every trace of oil, sand and pitch was sent flying from his fur; and after a brief pause, once more the pair mounted.

But now their mount was far more at ease, as if it knew that no dangers lurked in this region, and its pace was much slower as it picked a zig-zag path across a vast and boulder-strewn plain. For several hours they crossed the plain, until finally they spied a dim horizon of black cliffs. The cliffs soared up for thousands of feet into luminous, opaque and misty heights; and there, where the rocky plain met the foot of the black cliffs, the running thing paused and sank down to let them climb from its back.

With its strange snout it pushed them toward grotesquely carved ruins where they loomed tall in the overhang of the cliff, and then it turned and without a backward glance scurried away. The glow of the lightmoss which adorned its sides gradually dimmed as it sped back across the plain, presently to become the merest, flickering will-o'-the-wisp.

Hero and Eldin watched it out of sight, then turned to an examination of the deserted, prehistoric piles which stood mute testimony of some primal, subterranean civilization. There was that about the ruins which soon set the pair to staring about in something other than mere curiosity; for the place was like nothing so much as a complex of titanic tombstones and mighty mausoleums, as if they walked through some ante-diluvian graveyard of the gods.

In a little while, however, as they grew aware of the utter desolation of the place—its stark antiquity, which had known no intelligent inhabitants for many thousands of years—then their apprehension evaporated and they began to wonder why the running thing had deserted them here. It had actually pushed them in the direction of this centuries-dead city, as if telling them that this was what they sought; but what they really sought was a way back to the world of fields and sunshine and bright skies above.

"It looks like the running thing didn't understand Mathur Imniss after all," said Eldin presently. Hero grunted an inarticulate answer and pushed on through tumbled ruins to where a great cave gloomed in the face of the cliff. While Eldin sat down on a rock and contemplated the silence and desolation of the place, Hero went exploring on his own; and in a short while, echoing down to the older adventurer where he sat, Hero's cry of excitement brought him to his feet in an instant:

"Eldin, I think I've found it—the way to the outside world!"

"You've what?" cried the other. "Wait for me!" And he set off at a run, following Hero's footprints in the dust to the great and gloomy cave. He soon found the younger man crouching in the depths of the cavern, his face turned upward and lined with a frown of concentration. Even as Eldin puffed and panted and recovered his breath, he saw a smile spread slowly over his colleague's face.

"What is it, lad?" Eldin asked, casting about in the gloom with his eyes but seeing nothing. "I can't see a damned thing. What are you grinning at?"

"You're not supposed to *see* anything," answered Hero. "You're supposed to feel it. The breeze, Eldin, the breeze on your face!"

And now the Wanderer could indeed feel that breeze, a steadily gusting wind from some higher level; and giving a whoop he took out his firestones, tore a scrap from his already ragged jacket and struck sparks which soon turned to bright flame. The light lasted for a moment only, then died with the flame in a gust which overwhelmed both; but before that flame died the adventurers saw the stone stairs and the upward-leading tunnel whence blew that wonderful wind from more accustomed climes.

Now they eagerly scrambled forward and upward, entering the steep, rock-hewn tunnel and climbing its tight whorl of centuried steps. The only illumination was a sort of dim phosphorescence which sprang from the corkscrew walls, which were featureless except for the marks and gouges of ancient workmen. Up and up they went, and after a great deal of climbing thought to begin counting the steps.

At seven thousand Eldin sat down and started to swear and Hero followed suit. The echoes of their weary cursing came back to them over and over, gradually diminishing until they sat in silence. Then, when they had their breath back, Eldin was prompted to inquire: "Who the devil could have built such a staircase?"

"Possibly," answered Hero darkly.

Ignoring his friend's morbid turn of mind, Eldin said: "But I'm bone weary! Don't tell me we're going to have to rest on these damned steps—perhaps even sleep here—before we're to reach the surface?"

"*If* we're to reach the surface," answered Hero ominously.

"Damn me, but you're a real ray of sunshine, you are!" Eldin snarled.

In a fine temper of his own, Hero turned on him. "Save your breath!" he snapped. "You're going to need it. I'm not sleeping till I reach the surface, and then not until I find a safe spot to lay my head. Man, have you

no fear for what might be lurking here in this great well
of a staircase? I'm damned if I'll stay here when there
are green fields somewhere up ahead. Now come on,
let's get a move on."

For a further hour they climbed, more slowly now, tiring rapidly, and as they went so the phosphorescence
faded from the walls to leave them groping upward in
inky blackness. Since by now their eyes were fairly
well accustomed to gloom and darkness, and since there
was nothing to do but proceed up and around the tightly
spiraling stairs, Eldin refrained from burning anymore
of his sadly depleted jacket and simply followed in
Hero's footsteps. He did have one panted observation to
make, however, namely:

"S'funny, lad, but this is the first time I've known it
to get darker the closer we get to daylight!"

"I was thinking the same thing," Hero wearily answered. "Of course, it might be night up there." A moment later, he added: *"Owp!"*

"Owp?" repeated Eldin, stumbling upon him from
behind. "What's up?"

"We are, I reckon," came Hero's voice in the darkness. "But there's a lid on this damned hole and I've
just cracked my head on it. Here, come up alongside
me."

Eldin squeezed his bulk up beside Hero and gingerly
felt above his head until his fingers found the stone
door or plug which covered or filled the stairwell. He
gave it a tentative shove but was answered with total re-
sistance. Whatever it was that blocked the way, it was
solid and heavy. "We need a light," Eldin grunted, and
a moment later there came a tearing sound, the scrape
of firestones, sparks and a small crackle of flame.
Above their heads, illumined in the flare of yellow

light, a flat, solid slab showed its gray underside. But it *was* a slab, not a plug, and the pair sighed their relief in unison. At least they stood a chance.

Now, as the darkness returned, they bent their heads, put their backs to the slab and heaved. It gave a little, the merest fraction, then settled back. Sweat rained from the pair as they strained again; and again the slab moved, only to fall back firmly into place when they could no longer take its weight.

Hero stooped and found a rounded pebble. "Again," he said; and once more they strained and heaved. This time, as the slab lifted its customary half inch, Hero pushed the pebble into the gap. "Now we find a bigger pebble," he panted, "and so on." Except there were no more pebbles and they could not recall passing any on the way up.

After a moment's thought Hero took out his curved sword and fingered the rounded pommel and hilt. "Heave!" he commanded; and as the slab lifted he slid the inch-thick hilt of his sword into the gap. Now, as they rested for a second or two, Eldin took out his own blade and shoved its point slantingly up through the opening. He was rewarded with a shower of dirt, several worms, some tiny centipedes and grubs.

"Soil!" cried Hero. "And shallow soil at that!"

Eldin began to use his sword in a sawing motion, cutting through thick turf above until a dim beam of light dropped like a shaft into the miles-deep staircase. They began to work frantically then, lifting at the slab and sliding it, gradually moving it to one side; and in between bouts of straining they would saw and hack at the turf as the gap grew ever wider.

Then, after a small landslide of dirt and tiny scuttling things, putting every last ounce of their combined strength to the task, they again bent their backs and heaved at the slab. With a ripping of rootlets and turf and an even greater deluge of loosened soil, finally the slab slid to one side, leaving a gap through which they could scramble into the field above. There, side by side, they lay on their backs astounded by a darkening evening sky and bursting with gladness at the sight of wispy, slow-moving clouds. But their joy was short-lived, for in the next moment—

The stench hit them . . .

That awesome stench of death and decay and things long corrupted and fallen into putrefaction. The overwhelming fetor of the open tomb. They gagged, and if their stomachs had been full, surely that monstrous smell would have emptied them.

"Only one place in all the dreamlands could possibly smell like this," gasped Eldin as he turned green.

Hero nodded, his hands to his mouth and nose. "Right," he gagged. "Zura—and these must be the charnel gardens!"

The Aerial Armada

Beyond any shadow of doubt this was Zura. That fact was obvious now that the adventurers had time to study their surroundings. For quite apart from the smell—perhaps even explaining some of it—they saw that they lay in a field of diseased grass studded with leaning tombstones, and that the earth within each small plot had been pushed up from below! Oh, yes, this was that land where graves are unquiet and corpses noisy as well as noisome, and it reflected hideously the subterranean city of slabs from which the pair had escaped into this, its external extension.

Staring at the dark soil of the disturbed graves, Eldin dryly commented: "Big moles in Zura, eh?" But Hero only grimaced at his joke. Then the older man said no more but fashioned a pair of nose- and mouth-masks from his thoroughly ravaged jacket. Fastening these to their faces and tying them behind their heads, the pair were able to breathe more easily. Only then did they rise cautiously to their feet, improving their view of the place. What they saw was not reassuring. Their field of tombstones and open graves was only one of many, and endless rows of lolling slabs reached to a horizon of megalithic mausoleums whose morbidly carved columns reared into the sky and formed the ramparts of the city Zura itself. What did surprise them, however, was the apparent absence of life—or death, as Eldin had it.

"I agree," said Hero, "there is a strange dearth of death about the place—the mobile variety at any rate—though certainly I can smell where it's been."

"It's not where it's been that worries me," said Eldin, "but where it'll be next. I mean, what do corpses *do* evenings? Where's the night life in Zura? Or rather, the night death."

"Dunno," answered Hero, stretching. "Maybe they've all rotted away—or perhaps Kuranes figured out a way to finish them off."

"So where do we go from . . . *get down!*" Eldin hissed the final instinctive pair of words as, without other warning, a great slanting shadow fell over them. They dropped to their knees behind a huge headstone, turning their eyes skyward to gaze in awe and wonder at the flying ship which sailed slowly into view from high above the crumbling stone facade of a nearby mausoleum.

One ship, two, half-a-dozen—no, an entire armada of black ships under black sails—their octopus figureheads gazing balefully ahead through eyes painted the color of blood. And now the adventurers knew where the inhabitants of Zura the land were: manning the sky-fleet of Zura the Princess!

"Keep your head down!" Hero whispered his warning as the ships passed overhead in a silence more dreadful than a peal of mad bells. "If just one of her zombies chooses to look overboard at this very moment . . ."

But no one looked overboard, and the black ships sailed on with *The Cadaver* in the lead, high over Zura the city and climbing through rays of late sunshine into the evening sky. Their course lay to the west, their destination—

"Serannian!" Hero hissed, the short hairs rising at the back of his neck. "It can only be Serannian."

"She's going to do it," Eldin gasped through his facemask. "Shoot Serannian right out of the sky!"

"Unless we stop her!" Hero snapped.

Eldin's heart sank as he recognized the desperation, the frustration, the trapped action in his friend's voice. "Stop her?" he repeated the younger man. "Are you crazy?"

"Maybe," answered Hero, his voice hardening, "but that's what Kuranes hired us for, isn't it? I mean—can you really imagine what it would be like? Serannian, falling out of the sky . . ."

"But *how* are we going to stop her?" Eldin demanded. "She's already airborne—Zura and all her gang and her entire fleet. Like a swarm of great locusts in the sky."

"No," said a quiet, muffled voice behind them, causing them to snatch at their swords in a slithering of steel, "not her entire fleet. You were right, Hero—she's low on zombie-power. She didn't have enough corpses to man all of her ships. She had to leave one of them behind."

The adventurers had whirled at first sound of that muffled half-familiar voice. They had dropped into defensive crouches, blades outstretched and snarling lips drawn back from clenched teeth; but now, in a moment, their jaws dropped and their eyes widened in disbelief as a masked but recognizable figure stepped out from behind a cracked and leaning tombstone.

"Dass!" they gasped then in unison. "Limnar Dass!"

"At your service," Dass replied with a bow and a

sweep of his arm. "And delighted beyond words to see you, who I had thought never to see again."

"But how?" inquired Eldin, sheathing his sword and grasping the captain's outstretched hand. "You fell right off that damned volcano! We heard the rope snap."

"I fell a short distance, aye," Dass nodded. "And I banged my head on the way down. When I woke up it was morning and I was covered with a pile of small rocks and a layer of dust. There was no sign of you two. In the daylight it was easy to get down from the peak and I soon made my way to Baharna. I hired a fisherman to get me off Oriab and he put me ashore east of Zura. From there I made my way here on foot. All of this took a few days, of course. I've spent today hiding and watching the zombies prepare the fleet."

"But how come you stumbled on us right here, right now?" asked Hero.

"When I saw the zombies leaving the city to man the ships, I stole into the city and found the place where Zura makes her green gas. I took a vial of gas and was on my way back to the sky-docks when I heard voices. Since the zombies don't talk a lot I knew you must be human, and when I got close enough I recognized your voices."

"But—" Eldin began, and Limnar cut him short with:

"Listen, let's get back to the sky-docks. Now that there are three of us, maybe we can fly that ship I mentioned. I'm a sky-captain, remember? And on the way you can tell me how *you* got down off that volcano, right? But let's hurry. If we're going to do something about Zura, it will have to be fast."

He led them to an area where acres of massive blocks of stone formed a square raised platform, its surface covered with capstans, iron mooring rings and many coils of thick rope. In one corner of the platform a lone ship hung suspended in midair, moving gently from side to side in the evening breeze. The ship was moored fore and aft, port and starboard, and a rope ladder dangled from deck to platform.

Making their way across the sky-dock to where the ship was moored, the adventurers finished telling Dass their tale, and as they reached the ladder he made them the following offer. "Listen, you two: no matter the outcome of this battle between Zura and Serannian, when it's all over I would like to come with you in search of a shantak-bird's egg."

"You're on," said Hero at once.

"Damn right!" Eldin agreed, "but I still fail to see what the three of us can do against Zura. I mean, what's one small vial of green gas against her armada of ships with their holds crammed full of the stuff?"

"If we get to Serannian first," Dass explained, "perhaps Kuranes' scientists can manufacture the gas for themselves, or his magicians might be able to duplicate it there and then. Either way, we have to try. Incidentally, I'm pleased that you chose to continue with Kuranes' quest. You could have found plenty of other places to leave the underworld. I believe there are many such."

"Yes, well—that was sort of an accident," Hero coughed behind his hand.

"Accident or none, still I'm pleased," said Dass.

They climbed the rope ladder to the ship and went below decks. Because the ship had been blowing in the breeze, as it were, its odor was bearable. Traces of previous occupation still lingered below decks, however, but they were not overpowering. The three were able to take off their masks without undue suffering.

In the hold they found many hundreds of gas-filled cannon balls and great carboys of greenly swirling gas with unplugged balls ready for the filling. Dass took out his small vial and looked at it in disgust. "Well," he commented, "going into the city for this was a waste of time if ever there was one."

"You wouldn't have stumbled onto us if you hadn't," Hero reminded.

Dass replaced the vial in his pocket and they went back up onto the deck. "I reckon we can fly her," said Dass, "but only just. I had a look at her engine down there and it seems in good working order. Her flotation compartments are a bit smaller than on Kuranes' ships; that's because she needs the room for her armaments. You realize, of course, that we're going to have our work cut out? She's a big ship."

"Aye, we can see that," growled Eldin. "Ah, well, let's get at it. After all, Zura and her dead 'uns have an hour's start on us."

While Dass gave the ship a final check over, Hero and Eldin began carting flammable materials up the rope ladder and onto the decks. When the sky-captain was ready for shoving off, he asked them what they thought they were up to.

"Eldin has a thing about fires," Hero explained. "He likes to see places burn—especially places like Zura, the city. So, as we fly over that great tomb, we'll drop a few fire-bombs on her."

"Fine," Limnar agreed, "so long as you don't set fire to the ship as well!" After a moment's thought he added, "In fact it's a great idea. I noticed some axes in the hold. Why don't you get them out and do a bit of work above decks? There's a lot of unnecessary, very heavy woodwork up here. If we're going to overtake the armada and get to Serannian first, we'll need all the buoyancy we can muster."

Half an hour later, aboard a ship which looked radi-

cally different now—literally trimmed to the bone—the
adventurers sweated to carry out Limnar's orders as
their craft rose up and cleared the outer walls of the deserted city of the dead. And as soon as he gave them the
signal they were ready with torches, setting fire to anything that would burn and kicking the blazing masses
overboard. Down below the city smoldered at first, then
caught fire and finally blazed as the night wind took
hold of the flames and raced them uproariously through
the rotting streets.

Climbing higher into the night sky, they looked back
and down upon a city burning from end to end. It was
as if the wind had been waiting for just this
moment—as if all of the good old gods of dreamland
approved the actions of the three and were aiding them
in their efforts—for it now seemed that Zura's stones
themselves were burning, blazing up in a glorious and
cleansing mile-wide sheet of furnace heat.

Then they were up above the clouds and that mal-
odorous land was lost from sight, and high overhead the
stars of night peeped down in friendly fashion as the
black ship sailed into the west . . .

An hour before midnight, when the wind was steady
and the ship flew herself, Limnar sprang a pleasant surprise on the adventurers. In his bag he had a loaf of
bread, some cheese and a small packet of tea. They sat
together on the stripped-down bridge and munched hun-
grily while Eldin brewed tea with which to wash down
their frugal but satisfying meal. Afterward, as the adventurers leaned on a part of the rail they had found impossible to remove and watched the reflection of the
moon in the Southern Sea far below, Eldin asked Hero:
"What do you suppose will happen when Zura sees us
coming up behind her?"

"Umm? Oh, Limnar says we'll go far over the top of the armada. We're about a dozen zombies and a whole lot of gear lighter than the ships in Zura's fleet. He reckons we'll catch up, too, provided the wind doesn't change. In the morning we're going down to a couple of hundred feet. I'll fashion some fish hooks and there's plenty of twine aboard. We'll eat well tomorrow. Right now, though, I reckon you should get some sleep. I'll give you a shake in about three and a half hours, when it will be my turn. Limnar says he's been sleeping well and doesn't need it; but I know you're tired, and I certainly am."

"Say no more," said Eldin gratefully. He found a large coil of rope and curling himself up in its well fell asleep immediately, knowing no more until Hero wakened him. Using the same bed, Hero too soon fell into a deep sleep. And the night seemed to pass in a twinkling . . .

"Up, lad, quickly!" came Eldin's urgent growl as he almost dragged the younger man from his nest of ropes. "We've company."

For a moment, his mind given over to wonderful dreams within dreams—having forgotten where he was and what he was about—Hero was lost. Then, with the early morning sun striking beams of light into his eyes, he remembered. "Company? You mean we've caught up with Zura's armada?"

"No," Limnar Dass called down from the helm, "the Wanderer means that someone's caught up with us!"

"Eh?" said Hero, frowning. "What are you two going on about?"

"Look up there in the sky," Eldin replied. "Behind us—about a quarter of a mile and closing rapidly. Now then, what do you see?"

"I see—" Hero paused, squinting his eyes against the unaccustomed sunlight. "I see gaunts! Seven or eight of them."

"Ay," Eldin grimly nodded, "that's right. And if you look closer you'll see that one of them's an especially big bugger—and that he has a rider on his back!"

Again, Gytherik

CHAPTER XX

"That's Gytherik, said Hero. "He's somehow picked up our trail."

"You state the obvious beautifully," said Eldin.

"Not *our* trail," Limnar contradicted, "mine. He must have gone back to the volcano, saw my snapped bit of rope lying where it fell, picked up the trail from there. Actually, I thought I saw the gaunts over the shores of the Southern Sea before I set out on foot for Zura, but I couldn't be sure."

"Well, now you're sure," said Eldin. "And now we can tell Gytherik where his father is. That will release us from our pledge to Mathur. Gytherik himself can flap off and find his father a shantak-bird's egg."

"Or," said Hero, thoughtfully stroking his chin, "we can do a little trading with the gaunt-master."

"Trading?" Eldin was immediately suspicious. "What sort of trading?"

"Yes," said Limnar, "tell us more. What's young Gytherik got that we want so badly?"

"Gaunts!" Hero laughed out loud. "He's got gaunts—and they're five times as fast in the air as one of these damned ships. By the time Zura gets to Serannian, we'll have been waiting for her for at least a couple of days!"

"What?" Eldin's bull roar signaled his disapproval. "If you think for one minute that I'll—"

"Think?" Hero cut him off. "I damn well know you will!"

"Hero's right," said Limnar. "Kuranes needs as much time as we can win for him. I'm all for it. It's a good plan."

"Oh?" Eldin snarled. "And what happens if we tell Gytherik about his old man and he just hops back on a gaunt and leaves us here anyway?"

"We don't tell him till we get to Serannian, stupid!" Hero answered. "Anyway, here's the man himself."

Coming up fast from behind, a little higher than the ship's mainmast, Gytherik led his gaunts in a Vee-shaped formation. The youth's eyes scanned the deck of the black ship until he found the three where they stood by the helm. Now he gestured and his gaunts swooped down into the rigging and settled upon sails and ratlines, worrying at them in an attempt to disable the vessel.

"Hey, cut that out!" yelled Hero.

"Dammit all, you need us more than we need you!" roared Eldin.

"And that's the truth!" Limnar shouted.

"Gytherik," Hero yelled, "will you listen to me? We've found your father!"

And at last there was a reaction. Gytherik hauled his huge beast back up and signaled to the lesser gaunts to join him in the sky over the ship. From on high he called down, "What kind of trick is this, David Hero? What do you mean, you've found my father? You can't possibly have found him. Nor will I—until you're dead!"

"Wrong!" roared Eldin. "We know where he is, and we know how to set him free. In fact, we've promised to do just that. Now then, for the last time, will you talk?"

At Gytherik's command his great gaunt sideslipped and drew level with the ship's bridge. The rest of the gaunts flew off to a respectful distance. "Go on," said the gaunt-master, "talk—but it had better be good."

"All right, listen," said Hero. He crossed to the rail and leaned toward Gytherik. "As Eldin said, we know where Mathur is and we know what it will take to free him, but we also want something from you."

"Name it and it's yours," cried Gytherik, beginning to believe. "But only tell me where my father is. Tell me, and if you speak the truth you'll have no more trouble from me. But if you lie—"

"Hold it, Gytherik," said Hero, "you're in no position to threaten. Not anymore. If we tell what we know straight out, that's it. We'd never see you again."

"But that's what you want, isn't it? It's what we all want."

"Not quite," said Limnar from Hero's side. "We have a quest of our own, Gytherik. We have to get to Serannian before Zura and her armada. You help us and we'll help you."

"Zura?" Gytherik called back. "I saw her fleet leave Zura the land. What's she got to do with it?"

"With your problem, nothing," growled Eldin as he joined his friends. "But it's a problem for thousands of others. Zura intends to send Serannian and all her inhabitants plummeting out of the sky. Her reason: to strengthen her army of corpses, her zombie minions. After that—" he shrugged. "She'll murder all dreamland!"

Gytherik flew his gaunt closer. "And if I help you to

get to Serannian before her, you'll tell me where my father is and how to set him free?"

"That's the deal," Hero nodded, "yes."

"How do I know you're telling the truth?"

"Can you afford not to believe us?"

After a moment or two Gytherik shook his head. "No," he said. He hovered his great mount over the deck and reined in. The gaunt settled and immediately headed for cover in the shadow of a sail. Gytherik dismounted and turned to the three. "They don't like sunlight, my gaunts," he explained. "And they hate flying in daylight. Can I bring them aboard?"

"That will be all right," answered Limnar, captain of his black ship. "They can go down below if they like—providing they don't touch anything."

Gytherik called down the lesser gaunts and they all filed below, like a troupe of faceless pterodactyls. Now the adventurers could see the strain on Gytherik's young face, his visible weariness. "I suppose it's time I began to trust somebody," he said. "On my own, I'm aging a year every week! But what's all this about Zura and Serannian? Does she really mean to destroy that beautiful, sky-floating city?"

"She does indeed," Limnar nodded gravely.

"That can't be allowed."

"Our sentiments exactly," said Hero. "Do I take it then that we're agreed?"

"Maybe," answered Gytherik cautiously—and then: "Since I'm over a barrel, yes." He stuck out his hand. There were handshakes all round, following which Limnar asked if it would be safe to go below decks with the gaunts down there.

"By now they'll be fast asleep," Gytherik answered. "They won't stir unless you give them a kick, probably not even then. They don't make for good company, I assure you. Not just because they're unpleasant creatures; chiefly because they're boring."

As Limnar went below to attend to the buoyancy engines, Eldin said: "You've put my mind at rest no end, young Gytherik. I was beginning to believe you actually liked those rubbery horrors of yours!"

"Oh, you get used to them," the other answered. "But you may believe me when I say that I'd have no truck with them if they hadn't become necessary to my search. However distasteful, they're certainly handy as a means of transport. If we let them rest through the remainder of the day and bring them out at dusk, we'll be in Serannian by this time tomorrow morning."

"One thing," said Hero. "I counted eight little 'uns, and your big 'un makes nine. I was just wondering how we'll all manage?"

"My big 'un, as you call him, is tireless once he's airborne. He'll take me, for I'm used to him. The captain is tall but slight; the two smallest gaunts can take him. Two each of the rest for you and the Wanderer. That leaves two spare to spell the rest of the bunch. It should be easy—provided you wrap up warm. The way I see it, we'd climb to a high altitude and then simply glide for most of the way. The gaunts are good at gliding."

"Er, yes, we know," muttered Eldin.

"Eh?" Gytherik looked at him, and when no answer was forthcoming continued: "With the wind in this direction it shouldn't be at all complicated. We'll need to rig up harnesses for you that the gaunts can handle, so that they can change over without difficulty when they spell each other. Also, you'll have to put your trust in me . . ."

"What's that?" said Eldin sharply. "Oh, yes, that's right. For of course you could tell them to drop us right out of the sky."

"Why should he do that?" asked Limnar as he appeared from below decks.

"As a short cut to my father," Gytherik answered. "I don't blame you fellows for worrying about this. After all, I've already tried to kill you twice!"

"Listen," said Hero. "As far as I'm concerned those were pretty half-hearted attempts. You weren't giving it your all, else we'd be dead. Anyway, you've already proved your own sincerity by landing on this ship and placing your gaunts in our hands. And we've proved ours. If we were simply trying to trap you we could do you in right now."

"So if we all trust each other so much," said Gytherik, "why don't you tell me what I want to know? About my father, I mean."

"The temptation might be too great," Limnar supplied the answer. "You might just go shooting off on your own to free him. And we really do need your help. All Serannian needs it. By helping us—just this once—you can clear yourself of all other misdeeds. Namely, your attempts on Hero's and the Wanderer's lives."

"We're sinking," said Eldin, who had been silent for a while.

"That's right," Limnar agreed. "I've blown gas out of the chambers. Hero, did you make those fishing lines last night?"

"You've just reminded me how hungry I am!" Hero grinned. "Come on then, let's do some fishing."

The fish were biting and in a very short while several large ones were turning brown over a small wood fire which burned in a large copper pan in the center of the deck. With the flotation chambers filling again and the ship rising once more into the sky, the four sat down to their meal and made plans. Limnar, who perhaps had the greatest interest in saving Serannian, had most to say:

"I think," he started, "we all should take it easy today. Do some sleeping, take turns at the helm, have another good meal later tonight. In this fair wind the ship will continue to fly herself. We'll go for broke and see just how high we can sail her. That will save the gaunts. Then, tonight, when they've had their fill of sleep and darkness gives us cover, we'll scuttle this hulk and go gaunt riding. What say you?" And he looked from face to face of the others.

"We'll need to make harnesses," reminded Hero.

"And I'm not too sure I like the idea of the gaunts simply holding me aloft in a web of ropes," added Eldin. "Can't we tie the harnesses to their damned necks?"

"Uh-uh," Gytherik shook his head. "They'll need to spell each other, remember? No, I reckon Limnar is right. Our best bet is to get as much height as we can out of the pirate. Then the gaunts won't be flapping so much as gliding. That way they'll last much longer. In any case, they don't tire easily. But I do. Right now, I'm for a nap."

"I'll go along with that," said Limnar, rubbing at his eyes. "While we sleep the adventurers here can fix up the harnesses and keep an eye on our course and altitude."

"Right," Hero agreed. "We'll wake you in the early afternoon and get our own heads down. Then—"

"Then it'll be evening," Eldin rumbled ominously, "and we'll be placing ourselves at the tender mercies of Gytherik's gaunts."

"Don't you trust me after all then, Wanderer?" Gytherik chuckled.

" 'Course I do," Eldin forced a grin. And less cheerfully: "I damned well have to, don't I?"

Under False Colors

As the last rays of the sun illumined the sky to the west in a golden glow, so Gytherik mounted his gaunt and his three new friends climbed into their harnesses. All four of them wore parkas roughly fashioned of sailcloth as protection against the cold, for their altitude was now such that thin ice shrouded the rigging and their breath plumed in air which made the tiny hairs crackle in their nostrils as they breathed.

Two miles or more below them and some five or six miles to the west—like flyspecks on the golden, slowly closing window of evening—Zura's fleet forged for Serannian, and even at so great a distance that silent armada exuded its monstrous threat. And as Limnar had pointed out half an hour earlier, if they could see Zura's ships she could probably see theirs. Which was why, just before Eldin climbed into his harness to be lifted gently up and away from the frozen ship, he threw a fire-brand down into an open hatch.

Below decks things had been quickly prepared: oil intended for the engine had been splashed over coils of rope and the flotation chambers were pre-set to vent all of their mainly mythical essence in one mad rush.

When that happened the black ship would drop out of the sky like a comet, blazing as she went, and Zura would see her fatal fall. Then that Mistress of Death would worry no more about the lone pursuer and her unknown, unsung crew, and the mission of the four would be kept that much more of a secret.

And the plan worked to perfection, for indeed Zura saw the unknown vessel plummet to her doom—but she did not see the flock of gaunts (known collectively as a "grim") which came winging down the wind to pass high overhead in a long, swift, silent glide . . .

The armada was silent, too, and only a single, pale blue light—insubstantial as a death-fire—bore any testimony at all to its presence there in dreamland's night sky. That was the light from Zura's cabin on *The Cadaver*, where she now lay in the arms of a fresh lover . . . dead only a day or two from strangulation at the hands of a jealous husband. Zura had taken the liberty of removing his purple, protruding tongue, but there was little she could do about his glaring, bloodshot eyes . . .

And into the cold night glided Gytherik's gaunts, with their burden of shivering humanity clinging tight to frozen harnesses and setting their teeth against the windy rush of their flight. Mercifully, as the miles sped by and their altitude rapidly decreased, some of the numbness went out of them. Then a warm wind from the south found them and they opened their sailcloth parkas and finally discarded them, gray rags that whirled in the slipstream of the speeding gaunts before sinking in spirals and pirouettes to disappear in darkness.

Overhead the stars turned in their slow wheel and the moon arced like a slow, silver celestial discus from horizon toward distant horizon. And the hours sped by and

the glide continued; and strangely, the adventurers began to discover a fantastic exhilaration in their weird
journey across dreamland's heavens. They felt like great
nocturnal birds, masters of all the capricious winds of
night, and the pure joy of living rose up in them like
bubbles in champagne. Even their mission and its ut-
most urgency took a backseat to this sheer *joie de vivre*;
so that as dawn issued its first roseate gleam far behind
them, they actually found themselves despairing of the
coming day. They wished that their ride could go on
and on . . .

Then, in a faint dusting of light far ahead, they spied
that darker blot in the dark indigo of the sky, that half-
magical, floating mass of rock, flesh, blood, soil, myth
and miles-high adventure which was Serannian. Far off
as yet and below them, the night lights of the city grew
brighter with their steady approach, until it seemed to
the four that they sped toward some scintillant asteroid
frozen in a catastrophic fall to earth.

But frozen for how long? Zura would see that fall re-
sumed if she could—was on her way right now to do
just that—and who to say her no? Thoughts such· as
these sobered the fliers as the miles shortened between
themselves and the aerial city; and as dawn bloomed
more fully behind them so Serannian's lights seemed to
dim and her bulk loomed massive in the sky.

The wings of the gaunts were beating now, but beating tiredly for their glide was long ended and they had
flown for many a mile. Thus it was a weary throb of air
which first alerted the pikemen atop Serannian's walls
to the grim's arrival; that and the sight of their nightmare, prehistoric shapes growing out of the fresh risen
sun as they sped toward the legended sky-island. Ah,
but a change had taken place along that wall! Its once
welcoming turrets and embrasures were now battle-

ments in the fullest meaning of the word, where showed
the squat snouts and shining mirrors of ray-projectors
and the solid platforms and piled boulders of hastily but
sturdily constructed ballistae.

Limnar Dass was first to alight upon the wall, and as
he loosened himself from his harness so the challenge
came from close at hand: "Who goes there? Friend or
foe?" And from along the wall to both sides there were
cries of alert and the scrape of weapons hastily re-
aligned.

"Hold your fire!" cried Limnar. "We're friends. I'm
Captain Dass of Kuranes' fleet, and these men are the
King's agents. Aye, and even the gaunts are friends . . .
of a sort."

"Hold fire!" the cry echoed all along the wall as an
Officer of the Pike climbed up with three guardsmen to
where the gaunt-riders were dismounting. A thin dawn
mist hung over Serannian's walls, and the officer came
forward carefully through its swirly veil to stare hard at
the sky-captain.

"Dass!" he said. "Limnar Dass. Indeed it is you.
We've orders for you and your friends, Limnar."

"Orders?" Limnar clasped the other's outstretched
hand. "What orders?"

"That in the event of you and your friends returning
to Serannian, you're to report to Kuranes on the double."

Limnar nodded. "I expected some such. And I can
see that Lord Kuranes has not been idle in the last week
or so. Does this ring of armaments surround the entire
sky-island?"

"It surely does," answered the other. "Doubtless
Kuranes will tell you all about that when he sees you.
I'm sorry to be so abrupt and off-hand, Limnar, but or-
ders are orders. You're lucky that the Tilt is lying in

your favor; you can be with Kuranes in little more than an hour."

"Less than that," said Gytherik, stretching his limbs. "Just give the gaunts a couple of minutes to recover their strength—" he jerked a thumb at the faceless, rubbery creatures where they huddled together at the very rim of the wall, "and they'll be ready to take us on the last leg of our trip."

"A magician?" said the Officer of the Pike, warily eyeing Gytherik up and down. And as Hero and Eldin approached he added: "And a pair of wandering rogues! I've heard plenty about these two in the last few days, and very little of it complimentary. Strange company you're keeping, Limnar."

"If you've anymore insults, constable or officer or whatever you style yourself," snarled Eldin through his beard, "keep them to yourself. I'd as soon cave in your tin helmet as listen to anymore of your loose, uncivil lip!" He loomed over the suddenly silent captain and glared down at him.

"Easy, old lad," cautioned Hero, catching at his friend's elbow. "He means no harm, and we've no valuable time to waste in cracking skulls." He turned to the officer. "You run along now and, er, give your orders. We'll be on our way again in a minute."

"Er, well, yes—" agreed the cowering officer, staring upon into Hero's wild-seeming face; and he retreated with his men down stone steps and into a nearby bartizan.

Now the four stretched themselves and did a few warming exercises on the wide wall. The sun rose higher and the mist lifted, and the gaunts began to shuffle about uncomfortably as they felt the sun's rays warm on their clammy hides. Finally Gytherik said:

"Right, let's get on our way," and without pause he

called to his great gaunt and climbed up onto the base of its neck. "And when at last we reach Kuranes' manor house, then you'll tell me what I want to know, right?"

"Right," agreed Hero emphatically. "And after that it's up to you. If you want to stay and help us fight off Zura, fine. If not—well, we won't blame you. You can go off on your own and see to your father's rescue. And we'll all wish you the very best of luck. Actually, I myself wouldn't be so keen on the coming fight if I didn't figure that we owe Zura a bloody nose." His eyes narrowed.

"Damn right we do," growled Eldin. "And she'll be sorry she ever tangled with us, you may believe it. But it's not your fight, Gytherik. You must do as you think best. If you choose to go after your old man, well, that's your choice. Just make sure you give him our regards when you see him."

Moments later the grim launched itself from the wall and, with Limnar Dass taking the lead, rose into the sky over Serannian and set a course for Kuranes' manor house. And it was then that the sky-captain spotted something in the city's great harbor—something which caused him to call out:

"Down there, lads—look! That white ship amid the harbor's clutter."

"What of it?" Hero yelled back.

"Don't you recognize her lines?"

"I do," boomed Eldin, "and her Kraken figurehead!"

"One of Zura's ships?" called Gytherik. "Are you sure?"

"I'd know those lines anywhere," cried Limnar. Ships have been my whole life, remember? What say we go down and take a closer look?"

"We had better do just that," Hero agreed. "Kuranes

may not know it, but suddenly I've a suspicion he's harboring a viper in his bosom. A black one painted white!"

They zoomed down out of the sky and alighted on the white ship's deck. Hero freed himself from his harness and went to the rail where he chipped at the fresh paint with his sword. "Limnar's right!" he growled to himself as he touched the black surface beneath the white.

"And look at this octopus figurehead," boomed Eldin. "Even with its white paint and its sea-green eyes, still it's the very picture of evil!"

Limnar, who had been below decks, came up white-faced and trembling. Eldin caught hold of him and steadied him. "What's down there?" the burly adventurer demanded.

"Carboys of gas," Limnar answered. "Green gas! And bales of straw where other bottles have lain ..."

"Here now, what's all this?" came a gruff, official-sounding voice of inquiry from the gangplank. A stout little man puffed into view followed by half a dozen pikemen with their weapons at the ready.

"And who the hell are you?" questioned Eldin in his softest, most dangerous voice, his eyes narrowing as they settled on the glinting pikeheads where they were leveled at him and his companions.

Hero stepped forward to lay a restraining hand on his belligerent friend's shoulder. He knew that Eldin was close to eruption. He was like a smoldering volcano which suddenly rumbles and emits clouds of steam, threatening at any second to vent its fury over all who stand near. And Hero fully understood the older man's mood. So much had happened to them—they had triumphed over so many difficulties—and yet even now, when all should be plain sailing, still there were petty

obstacles to be overcome and fat, petty men asking pif-
fling, flatulent questions. And as Hero had correctly de-
duced, Eldin had just about had enough.

"Dammit!" The burly adventurer shrugged Hero's
hand away. "I'm cold, tired, hungry—and I'm bloody
angry!"

Before Hero could utter a word Eldin whirled on the
newcomers, his straight sword leaping into his hand to
shear cracklingly through six pikeshafts as if they were
straws. Then its edge came magically to rest—one
eighth of an inch from the little fat man's neck. "You,"
Eldin grated, his face split in a white, mirthless grin. "I
asked you a question. Who are you?"

"Ulphar," gurgled the other, his eyes threatening to
pop from his head. "Ulphar Oormell. I'm the
harbormaster."

"Well, then, harbormaster," Eldin growled, "call off
your dogs, and quickly, while my patience lasts." And
he glared at the pikemen where they had backed off
against the ship's rail.

"Now then," said Hero placatingly, getting between
Eldin and the soldiers, "that's enough fooling about for
now. Limnar, be so good as to tell these fellows who we
are, will you?"

Limnar quickly obliged and as the tension eased so
Eldin sheathed his sword. When Hero saw that his
friend once more had himself under control, he ven-
tured, "Great oaf! We're on their side, you know."

"I know it," answered the other. "It's just that I think
someone should tell them, that's all."

"Yes, well, Limnar's doing that right now," said
Hero.

"So there you have it in a nutshell," Limnar finished
his brief explanation to the still goggling harbormaster.
"Without a doubt this is one of Zura's ships, disguised

to get into port here in advance of her main fleet. Which means that there are spies and saboteurs already in the city. Now we have to get to Kuranes as quickly as we can. You'll excuse us?"

The fat man nodded, his jowls wobbling like jelly. "Of course, sirs, most certainly. And what's more, I'll fill this ship with guardsmen like flies round a pot of honey!"

"Oh?" Eldin cynically rumbled. "Well, just make sure they're less easily swatted than this lot. If not, Zura's dead 'uns will surely climb all over them!"

As Gytherik remounted his gaunt and the others got back into their harnesses, Hero asked of the harbormaster: "What do they look like, this vessel's crew?"

"A bit taller than average, white-robed, hooded, secretive, silent—and they come and go with their jars. I thought they were simple traders. Their papers say that they're priests of Kled."

"The Kledans are small brown men," Hero grimly answered, "and they have no priests that I know of. But you're right about them being traders. They trade in sudden death—and on a grand scale!"

Then the grim was aloft and the harbormaster had to turn his fat face skyward to inquire, "What if they return to the ship?"

"Have 'em killed!" Eldin roared down from on high. "They're dead anyway, but you can always try!"

Kuranes: Hostage!

CHAPTER XXII

Sweeping down out of the sky over the manor house, Hero once again noted the striking likeness of this part of the countryside to a bit of Old England. For this area was of Kuranes' own molding and had been modeled after an oft-glimpsed memory of his previous existence in the waking world. Like Serannian's wall, however, the ivied manor house too had undergone several ominous changes.

For one thing, striped sentry boxes had been erected on the four approach roads close to the garden walls; and for another, within the gardens themselves a small, temporary wooden barracks had been constructed to house the King's own guardsmen. And so by all rights Kuranes' estate should have been perfectly safe and secure. Except—

Except that as the gaunt-riders circled overhead they could see no sign of movement or life in the place—but they could see the still form of a uniformed guardsman, complete with pike and bearskin, lying crumpled on the cobbled road beside his sentry box!

As Limnar Dass alighted on the road and examined the stricken guardsman, the others flew directly into the inner courtyard. There, hastily freeing themselves from the gaunts, it soon became perfectly obvious to them that all was far from well. Something had happened during the night, something of which Serannian's common citizens, freshly waking, were as yet unaware. Indeed Hero and his friends were the first to stumble on the thing, whose mystery was very quickly and easily fathomed.

The gates and doors of Kuranes residence stood gapingly open; all of the King's men lay where they had fallen; signs of fighting were apparent in the great hall, where one of Kuranes' butlers lay dead in a dark pool of his own blood; but of the Lord of Serannian himself—not a sign.

"Kidnapped!" Eldin snarled. "Stolen away in the night by Zura's dead 'uns."

Hero found an unconscious guardsman in an inner room and slapped his face until he came to. "What happened here?" the young adventurer demanded of the dazed man.

"Happened? Why . . . I—" Suddenly the soldier's eyes sprang wide open and he tried to scramble to his feet, only to fall back weakly into Hero's arms. "The King!" the man gasped. "Kuranes—and those wormy, nightmare horrors that came for him. And the gas—"

"Gas?" Hero growned. "Green gas?"

"No, not green—purple. The attack came an hour before dawn. Small vials of purple gas thrown at the manor house from all sides and tossed into the barrack rooms. Some of the men lasted a little longer against the knockout effect of the gas, but they were the unlucky ones. Those *things* in the white robes cut them down without mercy. As I lost consciousness I saw Kuranes carried out of his room and into the garden mists. It was all so quick . . . So well planned . . .

Kuranes' security wasn't good enough ... Who would have thought Zura's forces would dare strike here, in the very heart of the sky-island?"

As he finished speaking, exhausted by the effort, the guardsman's head fell back and his eyes closed. His chest rose and fell in the steady rhythm of sleep. Hero stood up and stared at Gytherik and Eldin. The faces of all three were pale in the unnatural quiet of the place. Then Limnar Dass arrived with a relief squad of pike-bearing guardsmen.

"I met these lads marching down the road," he said. "They've come to relieve the night watch. It's my guess, however, that they'll have precious little to guard. Am I right?"

Hero nodded, then went on to relate the unconscious soldier's story. As he finished, the Officer of the Watch sprang to attention. "Right!" snapped that young man, a Lieutenant of Serannian's 3rd Company of Pikes. "The way I see it the King's been taken hostage. Very well—you, you and you," he picked out three of the men in his command. "Off you go, at the double, and get word to the authorities in the city. They'll know what to do. House to house searches and so on." As the three chosen men hurried off to carry out their orders, the lieutenant turned to Limnar and saluted. "Is there anything else I can do, sir?" he inquired.

"You can secure the manor house and grounds," said Dass, "and revive these comrades of yours, if that's at all possible right now. Perhaps one of them knows more about what happened here. For the time being we'll be making this place our headquarters, until we've worked out what we're going to do."

"One other thing," said Hero. "Let the City Councilors know we're back. They may have already been informed, but it's very important that we see them as soon as possible. We've brought news of Zura. There's a black armada on its way here right now, with Zura herself in command."

"Aye," Eldin gruffly added. "She's on her way all right. Coming to watch Serannian go crashing to her doom!"

Hero turned to his burly friend with a frown. "Eh, what's that? Surely she's coming to bring about the crash, not merely to watch it."

Eldin slowly shook his head. "No," he said, "I don't think so. She's coming purely as a spectator . . ."

As the guardsmen dispersed to their various duties, Hero took Eldin aside. Gytherik and Limnar followed in time to hear Hero's question: "What's on your mind, old lad? Something I've missed?"

"Something we've all missed," growled Eldin by way of reply. "Well, not missed, exactly. It's just that things have happened so fast we haven't had time to get it all together yet, that's all."

Hero and Gytherik continued to look blank, but Limnar snapped his fingers and said: "Damn me! I believe you're right, Eldin!"

"Eh?" said Hero.

"Of course!" Limnar continued to speak in exclamations. "The white ship and its cargo . . . and Kuranes a hostage . . . and Zura's fleet due to arrive sometime tomorrow morning, possibly at dawn. Yes, I can see what the Wanderer is getting at now."

Eldin nodded. "Ask yourself the real purpose behind that white ship," he said. "Sabotage has already been mentioned. Very well, just what do the zombies intend to sabotage? Where's the bulk of the green gas which was in that ship's hold?"

"Why, that's obvious," said Hero. "There's only one possible target for—" And in the next moment his jaw dropped and his face turned ashen. "Serannian's flotation chambers!"

"Right!" said Eldin. "That's the way I see it. Oh, we know Zura's armada is capable of shooting down a ship or two—perhaps Kuranes' entire fleet, though not without a great deal of damage to her own—but how could she hope to handle all of Serannian? Impossible from the outside, for the city's armaments are sound and the potential size of Kuranes' army is enormous ... but from the *inside*?"

"Where are the engine rooms?" Hero turned to Limnar. "They're below the surface, I know, but where *exactly*, and how many of them are there? Surely as a citizen of Serannian you'll know that much, Limnar?"

The sky-captain raised his eyebrows. "What? But I have no idea! Would you expect a taverner in Ulthar to know the intricacies of a silver mine in Ulthar's hinterland?"

"Well, who would know?" Hero pressed.

"The engineers, I suppose," Limnar answered. "They work in shifts. I've heard it said that some of the old-timers have worked on every flotation engine in the entire sky-island. As to how many engines there are: I believe the answer to that one is sixteen. But only four of those are master engines, monstrous great things that manufacture by far the majority of the flotation essence. The lesser engines are mainly for balance. They are there to give us the Tilt."

"So if Zura's gang is planning to take over the engine rooms—" Hero began.

"Or if they've already started," Eldin added.

"Their best bet," Gytherik concluded, "would be to infiltrate the master engine rooms."

"Right," Limnar agreed.

"I'm hungry," said Eldin after a pause, and the tension visibly eased off.

"You could use a bath, too," Hero told him, grinning as he wrinkled his nose.

"We all could," said Limnar reasonably. "We stink of gaunts."

"Me especially," said Gytherik ruefully. "Let's all eat, drink, bathe, sleep—generally refresh ourselves. But first—"

"The answer's an egg," Hero cut him short.

"Pardon?"

"The way to set your old man free," Eldin explained, "involves a shantak-bird's egg. That's what you wanted to know, isn't it?"

Gytherik eagerly nodded. "An egg, you say? Of the giant shantak?"

The adventurers took turns explaining and Gytherik listened intently. They told him the whole tale of their underground adventures, and when they were done there were unashamed tears in his eyes. Limnar had meanwhile roused a pair of Kuranes' butlers who had prepared a huge room for the four and were now seeing to a meal for them.

As they retired to their room Hero threw an arm round Gytherik's shoulder and said: "Well, lad, I suppose that as soon as you're fed and watered you'll be off to find yourself a shantak-bird's egg, eh?"

"Inquanok's hinterland is a fair way away," answered Gytherik after a moment's thought. "It will take a long time to get there and back, even using my gaunts. And they could use a good rest, I'm sure. Zura's fleet, on the other hand, is less than a day away, and the gaunts and I make a fine team in a fight. In fact, using the gaunts we can engage the armada before it even gets here."

"Are you saying you'll stay till it's all over?" Eldin gruffly asked, a delighted smile splitting his bearded face.

"I suppose I am," answered Gytherik. "I think my father would forgive me this one indulgence. There is one other suggestion I would make, however . . ."

"Oh?" said Hero.

"Yes. Do you think we could stable the gaunts closer to hand? Say—next door? I'm not a coward but I am discreet. The moment I feel this sky-floating island start to wobble . . ."

"I for one couldn't agree more," Eldin replied. "In fact, as soon as we've eaten I'll see to it myself."

An hour or so later—with all of their immediate needs satisfied and as they were about to stretch out on their beds in the huge room which they had made their headquarters—one of Kuranes' butlers knocked at their door, entered, bowed and announced the arrival of three of Serannian's councillors. Hero bade the three graybeards enter and the butler quickly produced chairs for them.

Introductions followed and the three newcomers turned out to be Messid Lythta, Allain Merrinay and Chelos Smith. The latter, as his surname might suggest, was a man late of the waking world who had lived for many years in Serannian. He suspected that he had been a policeman in the waking world, and if so he was a rare exception to a universally accepted rule; namely, it was almost unknown for a waking-worlder to follow the same vocation in the land of Earth's dreams. In fact Chelos (he had been awarded half of a dream-name) was not truly a policeman, but he did advise the City Fathers on what little crime there was in Serannian.

Messid Lythta was likewise useful, for he was the councillor in charge of Services and Amenities; he had overall control of the city's workforce, including its flotation engineers. As for Allain Merrinay: he was a personal friend of Kuranes'—and an expert on all matters concerning the sky-island's security. Three very important men indeed.

Though the councillors were old men they still had all of their wits about them. When Limnar Dass had finished telling them of Zura's approach, of the white ship, and all that was known of Kuranes' kidnapping, then the three went into a huddle together and conversed in lowered voices for many minutes. Finally they seemed to come to some decision or other, and Chelos Smith turned his grizzled policeman's head in the direction of the four where they sat on their beds.

"You are brave men all," Chelos told them. "We knew that even before your return, for the Lord of Serannian told us all about you. Now we are sure that he was right. Now, too, it is our intention to involve you in our plans for Serannian's security; also in the safe recovery of Kuranes himself, if he still lives. The way we understand it, however, you are all independently secure even in the event of the sky-island's fall. Is that so?"

"Aye," answered Gytherik, "for we have the use of my gaunts. I have but to call out to them and they would come instantly to our rescue."

"Very reassuring for you," said Allain Merrinay dryly, "but not very helpful to Serannian."

"Our plan," Chelos continued, "would deny at least two of you access to the gaunts—" and he gazed steadily at Hero and Eldin. "During the execution of that plan, if the sky-island should fall—you would also fall."

"Now hold on a minute—" Eldin started to his feet; but Hero only sighed and said:

"Sit down, old lad, for we're committed. You know it as well as I do, so we may a well hear the thing out." He turned back to Chelos Smith. "All right, councillor, say on—and let's hope for everyone's sake that your plan's a good one . . ."

Sub-Serannian

By midnight the groundwork had been completed and as much was known about Zura's advance troops as could be gleaned without actually entering their lairs. Those "lairs" were of course the subterranean (or sub-Serannian, as Hero had it) engine rooms which supplied the sky-island's cavernous flotation chambers with near-mythical, gravity-defying essence. The chambers themselves were vast natural and artificial caves buried deep in Serannian's heart-rock, from which the essence was vented as its efficacy waned. Some of this vented essence went to the air-baths; the rest was allowed to leak into the sky around Serannian, there to become one with that aerial Gulf Stream known as the Cerenerian Sea.

And so far Eldin's assessment of the situation had proved to be accurate; for through a system of covert surveillance organized by Chelos Smith and Allain Merrinay, it had been discovered that indeed the zombie saboteurs had infiltrated not only three of Serannian's four master engine rooms but also three secondary stations. They had been in complete control of these vital underground installations for some twenty-four hours;

but before that, as a coercive measure, they had kidnapped and made hostages of certain of Seranian's citizens—namely, the nearest and dearest of the flotation engineers in charge of the target stations.

Now normally Serannian's citizens were staunch and upright as any you might find in all the dreamlands, and had circumstances been otherwise and the enemy merely mortal the suborned engineers certainly would have found a way to fight back. Such was the love of the populace in general for Serannian that they would willingly give up their lives for the airborne city. This adversary was *not* normal, however, and the circumstances were quite extraordinary.

When a human felon takes a hostage as a means of coercion or for blackmail purposes, there is always the chance that he will eventually release his prisoner whether or not his purpose is achieved. Zura's zombies, on the other hand, had left no doubt whatever in the minds of their engineer victims as to what would happen to their loved ones in the event of their secret invasion being discovered. And because the zombies were what they were, the engineers were certain that if their wishes were not met, then that their loved ones were doomed. Who might bring to book someone already dead?

Also, while Serannian's citizens were aware that the city was threatened, Kuranes had not seen fit to reduce his fears to specifics; he had no desire to bring about wholesale panic among the populace. Thus, while the flotation engineers appreciated that the zombie infiltration of their plants must be part of some far greater menace, they were not aware of the exact nature of the threat. And so they carried out their duties as before, reporting for their shifts as required, and all the time hoping against hope that the zombie plot (whatever it was) would come unstuck and the threat evaporate. And after all, that was as much as could be expected of them if they were not to jeopardize the lives of their loved ones.

This had been their predicament as reported by Chelos Smith's surveillance crews; and now, as the midnight hour went by and members of relief shifts of engineers, in their sadly depleted homes, prepared in desultory fashion for work in their various underground plants, so Smith's and Merrinay's hastily mustered forces waited at the dark entrances to those scattered buildings which housed the elevators. A dozen men in all and hand picked, these were the vengeful forces which had been deemed fit to impersonate the engineers, to penetrate the flotation plants, to liberate the hostages and destroy Zura's zombies before they could perpetrate their acts of sabotage.

Twelve men forming six teams, one to each suspect plant; and as Smith had more than hinted, one of those six teams was comprised of David Hero and Eldin the Wanderer. Now, kitted out in clean white engineer's coveralls, they waited with Councillor Smith himself and two other stalwart citizens at the head of the shaft which fell to one of the city's main plants. And with practiced punctuality, fifteen minutes before the hour of Two in the morning, the genuine engineers converged despondently on the scene and entered the elevator building—immediately to be greeted by Chelos Smith.

"All right, you men," his voice called from the shadows as the engineers were about to enter the elevator's cage. "Take it easy—we know what's been going on."

Tired, nervous and edgy by reason of their predicament, the pair started violently and one of them dropped his bag of tools. They turned toward the five men who stepped forward into plain view. "What's all this?" one of them gulped, his Adam's apple visibly working, face white in the sudden beam of Smith's glowstone hand-torch.

"No need to pretend to us," Eldin growled. "We know your plight. How many hostages do the zombies hold?"

"Hostages?" the second engineer managed to get the word out. "Zombies? What are you talking—"

"Listen," Hero snarled, his chin starting to jut aggressively. He grabbed the two men by the loose material at the neck of their coveralls. "There's not much time. If you want to see your sweethearts and loved ones alive, just answer a couple of questions truthfully and with none of your flim-flam. We're not patient men . . ."

"For the last time," Eldin growled and lowered his scarred face to peer searchingly into the eyes of the engineers. "How many hostages, how many zombies?"

"Five zombies, four hostages," gulped the tallest of the two. "A hostage from each shift's family."

The other engineer grabbed at Hero's arm. "But wait!" he cried, his voice cracked and high-pitched. "You don't know what you're doing. These are dead men! They're cold, emotionless. You can't stop them. How can you hope to rescue our people?"

"We have more experience of Zura's zombies than you'd ever guess," Hero answered. "And we're not engineers, we're swordsmen." He tapped the pommel of his sword where it projected through the waistband of his baggy coveralls. "Also, we've studied diagrams of the plant. We'll be able to find our way about with no trouble at all."

"And you're wrong about the zombies, too," Eldin added. "They can be stopped. It's easy. You just behead 'em!"

"But—" started the taller of the two.

"No buts," Chelos Smith cut him short. "This is the

only way. Just hope and pray that Hero and Eldin here—yes, and all of the other fighters we've chosen to do the job at the other plants—just pray they can pull it off. Personally, I'm sure they can. Apart from these two, we've employed the greatest swordsmen in all Serannian."

"*You* are sure they can pull it off?" the engineers spoke as one man; and the smaller of the two continued: "You're talking about the lives of *our* wives, daughters—"

"Man," said Eldin gruffly, "we're talking about the life of Serannian itself—or the death of Serannian if we fail! But we don't intend to fail. While we're gone the councillor will explain the whole thing." He picked up the fallen bag of tools and stepped into the elevator's cage. Hero took the second bag from unprotesting fingers and followed his burly friend. The two turned and slid the door shut. They stared out for a moment through the door's metal lattice, then Hero pressed the down button.

As the elevator lurched and began to descend, Smith called, "Good luck, you two!"

They smiled grimly at his old face and Eldin answered: "Luck will have nothing to do with it."

Sinking out of sight, Hero added: "See you all in half an hour." Then the adventurers were alone and darkness filled the cage, and the square of light above them grew smaller as they fell toward the heart of Serannian.

At the bottom of the shaft two zombies waited, the cowls of their white but now stained robes thrown back to reveal heads from which black, dry flesh curled in strips to expose gleaming white bone beneath. The elevator worked on flotation essence and a gauge on the wall showed lowering pressure as the bottom of the cage came into view. The zombies moved jerkily forward, swords in hands, their hideous faces peering through the metal lattice of the door as the cage bumped to a halt. Beyond that lattice, the "relief engineers" stood with their backs to the door.

One of the zombies rattled the cage's door impatiently, then both of the dead men grasped at the external handles and yanked the door open. As they did so, the pair in the cage turned, stepped forth, swung their heavy bags of tools and released them in unison, then drew their hidden swords in a slither of whetted steel.

The zombies never knew what hit them. Knocked aside by the heavy bags of tools, they were allowed no time to recover. In a single moment their rotting heads were rolling and their twitching bodies toppling, and without pause the adventurers leapt for the door to the engine room. They threw the door open and hurled themselves through, taking in at a single glance the view that met their eyes.

Seated on the metal plating of the floor and roped to fat pipes that passed along the wall behind their backs, one matron, two younger women and a lovely girl, a mere child, huddled together. A zombie with a sword in his belt—arms akimbo, his cowl thrown back to reveal a face and neck alive with wriggling worms—stood guard over them. A second zombie kept watch over a pair of engineers where they worked, chained to the mountings of the great, throbbing engines. The third and last zombie was shepherding two more engineers toward the door—the very men Hero and Eldin had come to "relieve"—and in the center of the floor stood two medium-sized glass carboys of thick green gas, their stoppers firm in their necks.

For an instant the scene seemed frozen. Then as if time had been stopped briefly and restarted, everything came back to life. Perhaps, because of the very nature of zombies, the latter cliché is redundant on this occasion; but if death itself can quicken, then such was the case. The zombies recognized Hero and Eldin as strangers and therefore as a threat; the hostages, clapping hands to mouths, were likewise astonished but for the opposite reason; the weary engineers on their way to the elevator dropped into shocked crouches, their jaws falling open.

Then the adventurers were moving into action. As they sprang forward the zombie guarding the hostages started to draw his sword and the one behind the crouching engineers shoved them stumbling into the path of the bearded avengers. Eldin was able to knock aside the man who blocked his way and leap toward the hostages, where already their monstrous guard was lifting his weapon to use it on the helpless females. Eldin, seeing that he had no time left, hurled his sword with such force that he threw himself off balance and went sliding full length across the floor. His straight sword, however, flew unerringly to its target and slammed into and through the zombie's chest, lifting him from his feet and throwing him down.

Hero meanwhile had untangled himself from the still astounded engineers and was closing with their former guard. The latter, instead of attacking as he might well have done, had picked up one of the carboys. The jar was unstoppered now and its contents were about to be poured into an injection valve to one side of the throbbing engines. The third zombie had taken up the other carboy and was making for the door back toward the elevator. Hero's decision was therefore instantaneous; he hurled himself madly at the monster who threatened the engines.

And without the assistance of the chained engineers,

certainly he would have been too late. But even as the green gas began to flow thickly from the mouth of the carboy, so one of the men swung his chains against that jar and shattered it, filling the room with clouds of green gas and flying splinters of glass. At the same time his partner closed the valve, thus blocking any chance of the gas being forced into the city's flotation chambers.

By that time Eldin was upon the fallen zombie who had stood guard over the women. Avoiding the thrust of the downed creature's sword, he somehow contrived to yank his own weapon from its chest and hack at its head, which with his second blow flew free and so put an end to that particular threat. Hero, too, was engaging in a little swordplay; for as the gas began to disperse in the engine room, so the zombie at the injection valve drew his sword and turned on his charges. The engineers were still chained to the engine mountings and could not run, but Hero was not about to see them harmed. His swordplay was dazzling as he engaged the zombie, disarmed and neatly beheaded him.

Then, as Eldin raced for the door to the elevator and Hero saw to the freeing of the chained engineers, so there came that sudden, sharp tilting of the floor which told that not all of Chelos Smith's teams had been successful. At least one of the sky-island's engine rooms had been put out of action. The engines throbbed more powerfully yet as they fought to compensate, and little warning shudders seemed to run across the metal-plated floor in answer to the now uneven distribution of stress.

Now the engineers were setting free their loved ones, working in an almost surreal atmosphere of mixed elation and nightmare dread, still unable to comprehend their good fortune and yet filled with horror at the real-

ization that indeed someone was intent upon seeing
Serannian go crashing to its doom.

Then Eldin appeared in the doorway and his face was
grim. "I got him," he said, holding up his slimed sword,
"but not before he tossed his damned bottle into the elevator shaft!"

"Does that mean the elevator is out of order?" Hero
breathlessly questioned.

"Aye, I've tried her and she's not working."

The adventurers stared at each other for a moment,
then turned to the men and women they had come to set
free. And at last the tension broke and a babble of
voices began asking questions of the liberators. Finally
Hero was obliged to hold up his hands and demand silence. Then, to an audience that hung on his every word
with bated breath, he rapidly told his tale of Zura's plot:
how with the morning her armada of black galleys
would sail upon Serannian out of the east, and how then
she hoped to see the sky-island fall out of the sky.

"And depending upon the success or otherwise of
Chelos Smith's other teams," he finished, "that Princess
of Death might yet have her way. As for us . . . stuck
down here, as we seem to be for the moment, it's difficult to see how we can be of any more assistance."

"Oh, but we can!" One of the engineers started forward. "We can see to it that our engines work to their
very limits, giving the sky-island as much lift as they
can muster."

"Also," said another excitedly, "we can vent a little
essence into the elevator and clean it out. Within an
hour or so we should be able to get the hydraulics completely clear of that green filth."

And a third said: "That's the least we can do. If
there's a battle in the offing—and having seen the way

you two fight—why, it would be criminal not to make sure you have your share of the action!"

And without another word, with Hero and Eldin anxiously looking on but keeping well out of the way, the engineers began working flat out to put things back in order . . .

Swords of Serannian

Allain Merrinay was waiting with a full squad of pike-men at the top of the shaft when the elevator jerked to a heavily burdened halt. Then the door of the cage was thrown open and Hero, Eldin and their charges piled out into the terminus. Two of the engineers had volunteered to stay below and see the job through until relieved by the next oncoming shift, but everyone else was present.

When Merrinay saw them all it was as if a large portion of a terrible weight had been lifted from his shoulders. He congratulated the adventurers, said a few comforting words to the women, dismissed his guardsmen back to their stations atop Serannian's walls and then led Hero and Eldin out into the fresh night air. The stars were still bright above the city, but even so the sky held that hazy luminosity which warns of dawn's approach.

"What time is it?" asked Hero of Merrinay. His question said a great deal, for he was one to whom time generally had little meaning and was of even less interest.

"It's almost four o'clock," Merrinay answered. "Sun-up in less than two hours. And if you're right, that's just about when we can expect Zura to put in an appearance. Meanwhile, we have more immediate problems." He led them to where bicycles leaned against a wall and they mounted up. "Follow me," he said. "The Tilt is in our favor. It shouldn't be, but it is."

"That tremor we felt down under," said Hero as he drew level with the councillor. "That was one of the engine rooms going out, eh? We guessed it was."

"You guessed correctly," said Merrinay. "Which accounts for the Tilt being out of kilter. It was one of the master plants. Engines wrecked, pipes and the flotation chambers they fed filled with Zura's damnable green gas. The rescue was successful, however, and all the zombies were destroyed. We'll repair the mess eventually, of course—providing we're given the chance."

As they freewheeled through Serannian's streets, Eldin said, "But that's only one engine room, surely? What of the others? How did the rest of our lads perform?"

"Superbly," answered Merrinay, "with one exception. And that's the one that matters. That's where we're going now. Chelos Smith is waiting for you there, along with your friends Gytherik Imniss and Captain Limnar Dass. Smith has a plan—the craziest scheme I ever heard of—but he seems to think that you two can pull it off."

"Now wait a minute!" Eldin blurted. "Are you fellows never satisfied? Haven't Hero and I done enough around here? I mean—"

"I know what you mean," the councillor quickly cut him off. "And yes, you've done much more than we ever had the right to ask of you. But now—"

"Now it all hangs on us, eh?" said Hero.

Merrinay nodded. "That's right. As I've said, one master engine room is out of commission and will take days to repair. The other plants are back in our hands, with one exception. And that one just happens to be the biggest of them all. If it goes, then Serannian goes. Moreover, that's where Kuranes is held hostage—the King, and three women with him."

"What of the two men who went down?" Hero asked.

"A pair of fine, brave lads," Merrinay answered, then fell silent.

"So what you're saying," Eldin gruffly pressed, "is that we have to get into this last engine room, deal with the zombies and rescue Kuranes—and all before dawn?"

Merrinay nodded.

"Why us?" Hero asked.

"Because you're the best," said Merrinay.

For a long moment no one spoke. Then Eldin said: "Damn right we are!" And that was that.

To the bemusement of the adventurers, Allain Merrinay led them right through Serannian's nighted streets and almost to the harbor. They knew this area of the city and were doubly astonished when the councillor finally applied his brakes and dismounted outside the entrance to a certain establishment which they had used once before.

"The air-baths?" said Eldin with a frown.

Merrinay nodded. "I believe you're familiar with them?"

"We've used them," said Hero, "aye. Is this where we're to meet Chelos Smith and the others?"

At that moment the doors opened a crack to issue a copious cloud of warm, scented mist, from which Limnar Dass stuck out his head to stare at them. The worried look disappeared from his damp face in an instant and he gave a whoop of delight. His head disappeared and there came muffled shouting from within. Then the doors were thrown wide and Chelos Smith appeared, his hand outstretched in warm greeting.

Merrinay and the adventurers were ushered hastily into the reception room, where hurried hands began removing Hero's and Eldin's garments. The place was alive with pikemen, attendants, councillors and other dignitaries. Through the steaming vapors of an adjacent room, the adventurers were now and then able to catch glimpses of Gytherik where he stood talking soothingly to his gaunts; and seated on a bench was a trio of very handy-looking chaps, all naked except for belts and bandoliers of weaponry with which they seemed armed to the teeth.

While Hero and Eldin gazed mystified all about and as their disrobement continued, Chelos Smith explained what was happening. "These air-baths," he said, "get their essence from the master engine room where Kuranes is held prisoner. At least we strongly suspect he's there, for where else can he be? Anyway, doubtless Merrinay has already told you something of the problem. One of the master plants has been sabotaged, and if Zura's zombies cripple this one—" he shrugged helplessly. "It will be all over."

"But what are we doing here?" Eldin growled. "In the air-bath, I mean?"

"I'd say that this is our way in," Hero hazarded. "The zombies must have put the elevator out of commission. Now they're biding their time, waiting for the dawn and Zura's coming before—"

"Before they pump their green gas into the sky-island's main flotation chamber, yes," Smith nodded.

"Our way in?" Eldin continued to frown. "I don't follow."

"Of course you do," said Hero. "Since the essence

which supplies the air-baths is vented from the main engine room, we should be able to trace the duct back from—" He stopped abruptly and his eyebrows lowered in a black scowl.

"Now just hold on a minute!" He and Eldin were of one voice.

"It's not as difficult as it sounds," Smith hastily reassured the pair. "All you'll have to do is fight—which is what you do best of all. As for the rest: that will be done for you. There are maintenance men here who know every inch of the entire labyrinth."

"Labyrinth?" Hero was not reassured.

"Oh, yes. There's a veritable maze of great pipes and tunnels down there," said Smith. He gestured vaguely toward some indeterminate point underground.

"The more I hear of it, the less I like it," Eldin muttered.

"And you'll have three of the best swordsmen in Serannian right there behind you," Smith hurriedly continued. He nodded to where the heavily beweaponed trio sat waiting on their bench. "If you'd been five more minutes they would have gone without you."

"Well, that's different," said Eldin, beaming broadly. "I mean, let's not keep these good fellows back any longer." He cast about breezily with his eyes. "Just give us back our clothes and we—"

"Eldin," said Hero sternly, "you're wasting time!" And ignoring the groans of protest from his burly companion he turned back to Smith. "In for a penny, in for a tond," he said. "We're ready when you are. Just tell us what to do."

"Do?" Smith repeated. "Why, you simply follow the instructions of the maintenance engineer, that's all! My friends, after this you'll be heroes!"

"We already are," said Eldin. "What you mean is we'll be dead heroes, right?"

"Serannian will fall to her knees before you," Smith enthused, pretending he hadn't heard Eldin's remark.

"Or right out of the sky on top of us," added Hero darkly. "All right, councillor, you've made your point. Now let's be at it before we change our minds."

Smith called over a near-naked technician and introduced him, then gave a thumbs-up sign to the three fighting men on the bench. They stood up and joined the group, making rapid introductions. "Right," said the technician, a maintenance engineer whose job it was to tend the air-bath's flotation systems, "follow me."

He briskly led them through an arched doorway into the bathing area proper; that great misty hall with its huge, moisture-slick table of stone, festooned with safety-chains. This time, however, the adventurers were offered neither belts nor chains but led around the vast depression of the bath and into a private cubicle which bore this clearly marked legend upon its door:

KEEP OUT!
MAINTENANCE
ONLY

"The public aren't allowed in here," their guide explained. He pointed to a blue-tiled, seething well of vapor in the middle of the floor. "A man could fall down there and never find his way out again!"

"Oh?" said Eldin, directing his most powerful glare at Hero. "How very interesting."

"But you needn't concern yourselves about that," the man continued. "I've already seen to it that you won't get lost. You see this?" He tugged at a rope whose end was tied in a great loop about the neck of the well. "All you do is follow me along the rope. You won't see a lot because it's pretty dense and there are no lights. But there again we don't need lights. Just breathe easy and you'll be fine. If you feel like you're choking, don't worry about it. It's all in the mind."

"Oh, goody!" said Hero, feeling his throat tightening even as he considered it.

"No lights!" said Eldin. "I don't much fancy that."

"Oh, there is one light," said the maintenance man, "but that's at the sharp end. I've already put it in position so that you'll be able to see what you're doing before you burst in on them. Also to give your eyes a chance to get accustomed. Otherwise, emerging from the duct into the brightness of the engine room, you'd be blinded."

"That's all we'd need," Eldin grunted. "Blind as bats in G-strings and sword-belts. Ye gods!"

"That's it," the maintenance man chuckled. "Grin and bare it, eh? *Bare* it, get it?" Still chuckling he sat on the tiled wall of the well, swung his legs into the swirling vapors, turned his head and said, "Just follow on behind me, right? After you submerge, you'll find it easier if you go headfirst. You're weightless anyway so it doesn't really matter which end is up, if you see what I mean." And he ducked beneath the bubbling surface.

"Let's go," said Hero, and needlessly holding his breath, he followed on behind their guide.

Eldin took a last look about the cubicle and his glance met the steady gaze of the three swordsmen where they waited for him to make his move. "Well?" he said. "What are we waiting for?" He kissed the hilt of his sword for luck, slid the weapon firmly home in its sheath, swung his legs into the vapor and bumped from view—

—*And from then on it was hand over hand through*

swirling pea-soup, with the feet of the man in front just visible and nothing more, and only the distant throb of engines to match the rapid pulse of adrenalin-enriched blood.

The journey on the rope took all of an hour, some of it straight down and some of it along, around and even up. By the time they were at the end of it, the five who followed the maintenance man could not have said for sure which way was where. But of a sudden they were piling into each other and their guide loomed out of the tinted mist, his finger to his lips.

They were in a great pipe or duct all of five feet in diameter, and at this particular spot a glowstone lamp was fixed to the wall, its tired beam illuminating a hinged manhole about two feet across. Quietly, his voice barely discernible above the throb of the engines, the maintenance man began to speak:

"As you can see, the manhole's clamps are on the inside. That's so the manhole can't be opened accidentally from outside. If the engine room got flooded with flotation essence, there would be chaos in there. There *will* be chaos the second after you fellows burst in. You'll be fighting in free-fall, but at least you'll be used to it. Let's hope it works in your favor . . ." He paused. "It must be almost dawn outside. You'll have to hurry." His hands reached tremblingly toward the clamps . . .

There were six of Zura's zombies in that all-important engine room. Six zombies, three female hostages, three frightened engineers (for the fourth had been brave and foolish and was now dead) and one King, the Lord of Serannian himself. The layout of the plant was more or less the same as all of the others; the engines were slightly larger and their pumps massive. There were two large injection valves, both of them open in readiness, and seated on the metal floor at the foot of each were carboys of green gas.

The engineers, chained to the engines, sweated at their work; the zombies patrolled in pairs, restlessly to and fro, their swords at the ready. The elevator cage had been dragged from its mountings and was jammed firmly half in, half out of the shaft, forming a makeshift prison for Kuranes and the women. Its doors were chained shut and Kuranes stood with his hands tightly clenched on the lattice of diagonal bars. The door to the engine room being open, the Lord of Serannian had a clear view of most of the plant. In one corner, three bodies formed a haphazard pile . . .

This was the scene immediately prior to the entry of the rescue squad . . . the scene immediately thereafter was something entirely different. Kuranes was witness to the whole thing, and afterward he would readily admit that he quite simply could not believe the evidence of his own eyes.

The curve of a great pipe where it bulged from the wall suddenly fractured with a metallic squeal. A circular scab or flap of metal, the manhole cover, flew clangingly open, admitting a billowing cloud of gray-green, essence-filled vapor. Then there were strangers in the engine room—and more of them by the moment— near-naked strangers whose swords were flickering snake-tongues of steel.

No, not strangers. Even through the gushing, rapidly thickening mist Kuranes instantly recognized the style of at least three of these men from nowhere. They were weapon masters, instructors from his own military academy. As for the other two . . . there could be no mistaking them!

David Hero the one, Hero of Dreams, like some youthful, zestful god of dreamland's earliest days—a god with the cold grin of a demon as his curved Kledan steel severed the gray and leathery neck of a fatally astounded zombie! Eldin the Wanderer the other—that great, scarfaced ape of a man, roaring his fury in a voice that drowned out even the throb of the mighty engines—his straight sword biting through the rotting wrist of an already dead man even as that animated corpse reached for one of the deadly carboys of green gas!

After that, all was glorious mayhem and madness . . .

Vented!

CHAPTER XXV

Madness and mayhem!

Madness in the crazy way that everything suddenly became weightless; mayhem in the absolute abandon with which the avenging five hurled themselves into the attack on Zura's dumbfounded zombie cohorts.

An incredible vista opened to Kuranes' eyes, as of some alien, fog-wreathed Tartarean landscape, demon-inhabited and now invaded by silver-limbed airborne forces from some fantastic higher realm. And as the volume of flotation essence increased in the engine room, so its effect became that much more grotesque. Both mist and fighting quickly spread into the elevator room, terrifying the women in their prison cage but at the same time affording Kuranes a clearer view of some of the hand-to-hand combat.

A cartwheeling crush of arms and legs rolled slowly by in midair, leprous gray limbs entwined with healthy white; and rotting fangs were bared in menace against grim, firm-jawed determination. A zombie head bounded from nowhere, spinning like a Catherine wheel and spilling maggots as it caromed from wall to wall. Free-floating, detached limbs twitched as they were knocked about by the combatants; and the mounting sound of clashing swords, of savage cries, harsh breathing and throbbing engines rapidly grew deafening.

Then Kuranes caught sight of something which caused the breath to catch in his throat and chilled him to the marrow. Floundering about in the misted entrance to the engine room, intact and uninjured, a zombie gropingly sought to fasten upon one of the carboys of green gas, which spun and floated free in the air mere inches from its eager hands! Hero had also seen the danger, however, and now he came wriggling and kicking into view like some merman of ancient myth. He swam in through the doorway and sought to catch hold of the zombie's ankle, but—

In the very next moment the zombie grasped the neck of the carboy and somehow contrived to turn on his pursuer. Hero, off balance, found himself thrown against the wall, all of the breath knocked out of him, his curved sword flying from his hand. Seeing his helpless condition, the zombie reached for his throat.

Though Kuranes' eyes were riveted upon Hero's predicament, still his other senses took in all that was happening. He was aware of a lessening of the general din, and of someone—an engineer, he thought—shouting instructions. Something about the injection valves ... how they must be closed immediately. Then—

—The zombie took hold of Hero's throat with one hand, and with the other it brought the heavy carboy arcing toward his head. Coming to his senses in the nick of time, Hero somehow managed to duck beneath the blow and the carboy shot from the zombie's fingers and passed harmlessly over his shoulder. At the same time Eldin came diving in through the doorway, took in the scene at a glance and struck one final, killing blow.

As the zombie's head leapt from its neck, so the hurtling carboy crashed into the wall and shattered. Green gas immediately billowed up, expanding and filling the entire plant in a matter of seconds. There were astonished cries, loud clanging sounds, thuds and groans as gravity returned and floating men and materials regained their normal weight and fell back to the metal floor. Then someone thought to turn up the ventilation system and the green gas rapidly began to dissipate.

Moments later, after a rapid and very satisfactory head count (of both living and detached heads alike!) Hero made his way unsteadily to the cage of the elevator. He nursed a great lump on his head—where he had landed when the green gas was released—and several lesser bruises on his back, but apart from these superficial injuries he was unhurt. Eldin was already at the cage, straining at the chains where they held the door shut. Then one of the three weapons masters came forward with an engineer's bag of tools. He rapidly cut through the chains and the cage door was opened.

Kuranes, stepping shakily from the cage, hugged each of the five near-naked men in turn, then demanded to know what was happening and how Serannian fared. While the rest of the team tidied up and tended their mainly minor cuts and scratches, Hero quickly outlined the situation for the King. When he was done, Kuranes said:

"But I must get back to the surface as quickly as possible. We all must. I want to see how Serannian fares against Zura's armada. Damn it—I want to be part of it!"

"I don't see how that's possible," Hero answered. "The elevator is out of order for now, and we had to come down through an essence duct. It was unpleasant and it took us all of an hour. That's all very well for us young 'uns, but—"

"But there's another way," said a lively voice from behind the pair. They turned to look at the owner of the voice and Hero clapped the newcomer on the shoulder.

"This is the maintenance man who brought us down here," he explained to Kuranes. To the other he said, "You came through the fighting unscathed, I see."

"I wasn't part of it," came the answer. "I'm no swordsman. No, I stayed in the duct. But now that it's all over—"

"And you say there's another way out?" Kuranes eagerly grasped the man's arms.

"Yes, your Majesty, there is. That was my job, you see: to get these fellows down here, and then to get them out again. And the way out is a sight faster than the way in, I can tell you!"

"Explain," Eldin gruffly demanded as he joined the group. "What is this exit you're talking about, another duct?"

"More a vent, really," answered the maintenance man. He led them back into the engine room and across to the manhole cover, which was now clamped shut with a special tool. "This is a duct," he said, rapping the bulge of the great pipe with his knuckles. "That's the way we came in. This, on the other hand—" and he crossed the floor to the opposite wall and pointed to a similar manhole with a single clamp, "is an inspection tunnel. It leads to the great shaft through which all of Serannian's excess essence is vented to the surface. Fortunately it's the central shaft; it goes almost vertically to the surface. The shafts from the lesser plants all connect with this one at different levels."

"So what you're really saying," said Hero, "is that we're to go along the inspection tunnel and into the shaft—"

"—Where we'll float up to the surface?" Eldin finished it for him.

"Er—not quite," answered the other. "When I go into the tunnel in the course of my work, I wear a harness and chains. You won't be equipped like that. Down here, you see, where the essence is most concentrated, it imparts a tremendous bouyancy. No, you won't float—you'll shoot!"

"We'll shoot," repeated Eldin with a single curt nod. "Yes, well, that was a good idea. Now let's hear a few more."

"I see," said Hero, stroking his chin. "So in fact we'll be sucked out of the tunnel and hurled aloft . . ."

"Right," said the maintenance man.

"And where will we emerge?"

"I can answer that one," said Kuranes. "The orifice is a huge natural crater just outside the city. It's quite a spectacular sight when the engines are venting. You get a varicolored spray that goes up hundreds of feet into the air over Serannian."

"Hundreds of feet!" Eldin could contain himself no longer. "And after that, I suppose, anything sucked up comes down again—hard."

"Right again," said the maintenance man with a grin. "But we've thought of that, too. You'll be in good hands, believe me." He unclamped the manhole and opened it with a loud clang.

"Damn me," said Eldin, scratching his beard. "Maybe I'm a madman but I really do believe you! Well, say on, my friend, while we're still daft enough to hear you out. But watch what you say, eh? I'm sure my nerves won't stand much more!"

Circling high in the dawn sky to the north of the city, Gytherik sat astride the neck of his great gaunt and looked toward the east. There, beyond the sky-island's rim, war already raged across a broad expanse of the Cerenerian Sea. Zura's armada had been spied in the east an hour ago, and Serannian's fleet had immediately sailed to meet and engage her. From where he circled above the mighty blowhole, Gytherik could plainly hear the boom of Zura's cannon and see the bright flashing beams of Serannian's less than effective ray-projectors. And already the aerial ocean was stained green where it lapped the sky-island's rim, green-tinted with the taint of Zura's gas.

Even as the gaunt-master watched, he was sickened by the sight of one of Kuranes' ships—already holed, listing badly and clearly out of the fight—shuddering under a further battering from a pirate's cannon before spiraling down out of the sky. In the next instant, however, Gytherik was standing in his tiny saddle and cheering wildly. A gout of flame had erupted on the deck of a pirate and was devouring her sails and rigging. Blazing zombie figures fell like fiery ants from her roaring deck.

Gytherik knew what that burning ship signified: namely that half of his grim of gaunts had joined the fray. Serannian's chemists had been at work all night manufacturing firebombs: fragile bottles of incendiary liquid which the gaunts could carry in their prehensile paws and drop on the decks of the black ships. Four gaunts had been instructed in this tactic and were now beginning to employ it to devastating effect. A second ship burst into flame even as the first capsized and went plummeting to her doom.

Gytherik watched the battle a moment longer, cast worried eyes far to the east, then breathed a sigh of relief. Though the sun was up, its beams were as yet hidden behind great banks of distant cloud. When those clouds dispersed or blew away, then the gaunts would run for cover. That would be a great pity and a great loss, for the gaunt-master could clearly see how his rubbery allies were causing Zura a great deal of concern. Two more ships were beginning to burn and smoke was now curling into the sky from all quarters of the battle.

Then Gytherik felt a sudden uprushing of air, as if his mount had glided into a warm thermal, and his mind quickly returned to more immediate matters. He had been told that he would receive just such a warning before the great venting which would hurl his friends into the sky. Well, the warning had come and now he was ready. He called to his three free-flying gaunts and indicated that they should prepare themselves and be alert.

Nor had they any time to spare, for no sooner had the gaunts positioned themselves equidistant in their circling than the crater gave a great belch and blew clouds of dust and pebbles high into the sky. That heralded the beginning of a long, continuous and rapidly increasing exhalation of variously tinted, mildly scented essence, a column of shimmering vapor that shot like some ethereal geyser high into Serannian's atmosphere. And at the very height of that mighty mechanical snort, out from the crater hurtled a trio of semi-naked figures whose bodies turned in the air like a troupe of tumblers in a circus.

These were those master swordsmen, the instructors from Kuranes' military academy; and as they reached the meridian of their flight, passed out through the geyser's shimmering well into normal air and began to fall back, so Gytherik's gaunts darted in like great kingfishers to snatch them from mid-air and transport them in a series of dizzy swoops down toward Serannian's bastion walls. Though there was only one gaunt to each man, the flights this time were of such short duration—and all "downhill"—that the gaunts found little difficulty in remaining aloft until their charges were safely deposited.

And this time Gytherik's cheering was as lively and lusty a sound as ever that youth had uttered; for the emergence of the three weapons masters, unhurt and on time as scheduled, told him that the counterattack on Serannian's most important flotation plant had gone without a hitch. He knew now that it would be only a matter of seconds before the next eruption coughed up Hero, Eldin and—if he still lived—Lord Kuranes of Serannian himself.

And indeed as the lesser gaunts rejoined him where he rode the rim of the aerial spout, so there came again that warning belch from the black throat of the crater, and again the mounting column of essence like some mythical geyser of the gods. More powerful than before, the vented essence rose even higher into the sky; and in another moment, tumbling aloft like ping-pong balls in a fountain—

"Go get 'em!" yelled Gytherik to the gaunts, but his prehistoric pets had required no such instruction. With an independence most uncharacteristic of their kind, they zeroed in on their targets and snatched at them where they emerged from the rising column of shimmering essence.

Hero, feeling rubbery paws grasp him firmly under the armpits, hung on for dear life and closed his eyes against the nauseous spinning on his battered senses. Kuranes too clung grimly to leathery limbs where he dangled beneath frantically beating bat-wings.

And as for Eldin—

"Hero!" came the Wanderer's vibrating bull roar. "Hero, damn you! Hell's teeth—will you *look* at me when I'm shouting at you?"

Hero looked—Kuranes, too—and as they zoomed dizzily down and across Serannian's skyline of spires and steeply sloping rooftops, so they joined Gytherik in uncontrollable, near-hysterical laughter.

For Eldin's gaunt had caught him by the legs! And heedless of life and limb—dangling in that singularly undignified position—the Wanderer heartily, systematically and indiscriminately cursed the creature, its master, Hero, Kuranes, Serannian, Zura and all of the dreamlands as he was rushed without pause toward the sky-island's ballistae-burdened walls . . .

Again, Curator

Set down beside the sky-island's walls close to the great harbor, the three had an excellent view of the battle. Gytherik's gaunts were already taking a terrible toll of Zura's ships, and now the gaunt-master sent the rest of the grim about their inflammatory duties. The black armada now numbered less than seventy ships, and Zura must surely be wondering what had become of her zombie saboteurs.

Or perhaps she had already guessed that her plot was discovered and her saboteurs liquidated. Perhaps sheer rage or madness prompted her to proceed with her attack. For now her ships were arrayed in a line all along the rim of the sky-island, their cannons turned inland, and as at a signal there came a concerted booming and shots began to pour into Kuranes' ships where they stood between Serannian and the invaders.

The effect of these massed salvoes was devastating. Those ships caught in the withering blast shuddered, keeled over, issued vile green gas from their shattered hulls and slid silently out of they sky. Many a brave sky-captain went down with his ship in this way, and the shores of dreamland's lower realms would be scattered with grim relics of the aerial battle for many months to come.

Zura's cannons were also making their mark on the sky-island itself; for wherever her zombie marksmen missed their targets, still the shots smacked into Serannian's pink marble walls or passed over them to whistle on into the city. Everywhere the green gas roiled, and as buildings crashed into rubble and the screams of the dying mounted amidst the roar of battle, so Kuranes was beside himself with rage and sorrow.

By now the sun was well and truly up and its rays were warm on the beleaguered city. Gytherik, crouching in an armored bastion with Kuranes, Hero and Eldin, shook his head worriedly as his gaunts set out upon yet another foray. Tired now and weighted down with nets of firebombs, the weird creatures seemed visibly to flinch as the sunlight fell upon their clammy heads. The smallest of the beasts, flying far too low over the deck of a pirate, died in a tongue of fire from one of its own bombs.

Seeing this, Gytherik said, "They can do no more. The sun will quickly dry them out. Lord Kings, I'm afraid you've lost their services. This must be their last run. See how badly they fly, so leaden and weary-looking?"

Gytherik was right, but even so the gaunts put everything they had into their last assault. The sky rained fiery destruction on Zura's ships until the Cerenerian Sea was aglow with incandescent hulks. Then, through a drifting screen of smoke, the observers saw a brave sight. One of Kuranes' ships—sails tattered, hull leaking green gas from half-a-dozen gaping holes and decks a tangle of shattered timbers—bore down upon a pirate, obviously intending to ram the black ship.

"Is that *The Gnorri*?" gasped Kuranes.

"Aye," Eldin slitted his eyes against the drifting smoke. "That's the name she bears, brave ship."

"That's Dass!" Kuranes cried. "*The Gnorri* is his ship. He's bound to go down with the pirate!"

Hero grabbed Gytherik's arms. "The gaunts," he shouted above the renewed roar of battle. "Gytherik, can they make one more pass? Can they put us aboard *The Gnorri*?"

"What?" Gytherik yelled back. "Are you mad? Why not let them take Limnar off?"

"Because he might not want to come," Eldin gave the answer. "Not until the fighting's done. Look—" And he pointed out over the sea.

The Gnorri ploughed into the pirate and stove in her side, both ships locking together as timbers snapped, decks buckled and sails came crashing down. In the next moment a horde of zombies went swarming aboard *The Gnorri*, milling about a small knot of defenders at the base of her shattered mainmast.

By now the gaunts were back, landing on the wall close to Kuranes' command bastion, and Gytherik cried: "One more flight then, I agree—but only if I can come with you!"

"You're, on," yelled Hero. "Let's go!"

The three climbed up onto the wall and Gytherik called to his gaunts. Moments later they were airborne, with the gaunt-master riding his great mount and each of the adventurers suspended between two of the lesser creatures. Not to be outdone and despite their obvious discomfort in sunlight, the rest of the gaunts accompanied the main body of the grim out to the crippled ships. And down they flopped onto the littered deck of *The Gnorri*, landing awkwardly among the debris of rigging and shattered timbers. Dismounting, Gytherik hastily waved the gaunts back toward the stern of the ship and ordered them to wait there. He turned from this task in time to catch a sword tossed by Eldin.

"I hope you can make better use of it than he did," the Wanderer grimly commented, kicking at a headless zombie corpse. "Right then—let's be at it!" And the three rushed at the backs of Zura's maggoty minions where they hacked away at *The Gnorri*'s brave defenders.

Only two of the latter remained on their feet now, bloodied and battered but still defiant, and one of them was Limnar Dass. His face lit up like a lamp as the three newcomers smashed into the backs of the remaining zombies, and now Limnar was able to witness at first hand the sword-wizardry of these adventurers he was proud to call his friends.

But while Hero and Eldin were marvelous to watch, Gytherik, too, took his toll of Zura's zombies; so that the deck about the shattered mainmast was soon littered with dismembered and beheaded corpses. Sadly, even as Hero hacked the head from the last invader, so that creature's word struck the life from the man at Limnar's side. Then it was over and the deck beneath their feet gave a warning, shuddering lurch as the locked hulls began to sink into the green-stained Cerenerian.

Gytherik hastily called up his gaunts, and as *The Gnorri* and her victim fell from the sky the grim carried its human charges safely back to Serannian's wall. There they landed behind a screen of drifting smoke, and as a tearful Kuranes hugged his brave sky-captain, so there came a totally unexpected diversion.

At the eastern extreme of the sky-island, several of Zura's ships were blazing away at the Museum where it perched on its rugged promontory. This had been going on for some minutes when suddenly, from a ground floor window, a pencil-slim beam of golden light struck out and across the smoke- and gas-wreathed Cerenerian. For a single instant only, that beam played upon its pirate target—which then capitulated in a ball of white-hot fire!

And out from his Museum strode the Curator, clanking across the causeway, pausing now and then to gaze curiously, perhaps angrily at Zura's black vessels. And each time he paused, so a hot yellow gleam would come into his crystal eyes and the golden ray would strike forth, and another pirate would evaporate in a glaring white flash. Never once did he strike at Kuranes' ships, for they had not threatened the Museum. But as for the invaders—

All along the wall strode the Curator, cheered on by Serannian's defenders, his clanking footsteps echoing a final doom on Zura's mad schemes. And whenever he paused to look out across that fantastic ocean of the upper air, so the golden beam would strike out at the invader's heart, until soon only a handful of black ships remained. These fell at last under a concerted hail of boulders from dozens of ballistae, and only then did the Curator turn on his metal heel and make his way back to the Museum.

The battle was over, and away across the sky a lone pirate turned tail and set course for the east. Kuranes saw the running ship and placed his spyglass to his eye. *"The Cadaver,"* he said.

"Zura!" snarled Eldin. "Is the witch to escape, then?"

Kuranes turned sad, wise eyes upon the Wanderer. "Aye," he said, "let her go. Life to such as that Priestess of Darkness must be far more monstrous than any death we could ever devise." No one could deny the King this final sentiment, and with that the thing was over ...

* * *

At noon Serennian's dignitaries and as many of the city's ordinary citizens as possible crowded themselves into the great Hall of Proclamation, which stood at the city's center. Kuranes had many immediate honors to confer. Later, when sufficient time had elapsed for the collection and corroboration of various tales of heroism, there would be many more. Alas, too many of the latter would be posthumous; but for the present, the majority of today's recipients were very much alive.

First were the members of Chelos Smith's rescue teams (all of whom, with two sad exceptions, were present) and also the councillors who had masterminded the mission, Smith himself and Allain Marrinay. There were the chemists whose firebombs had been used to such devastating effect, and the designers of the ballistae on the walls, now in the early stages of dismantling. Many awards and honors, taking up a good deal of time in their conferring.

Hero and Eldin were there (strangely shy now that their heroics were about to be made public), Limnar Dass and Gytherik Imniss, too. Indeed, the latter had already collected one set of ribboned medals—for Conspicuous Bravery—on behalf of his gaunts! The legend of dreamland would never again be the same once the word had spread abroad that gaunts were not necessarily the nighted things of dark myth which they had always been supposed. No, it all depended upon who directed them.

Finally it was the turn of the adventurers, Hero and Eldin themselves, stepping awkwardly forward to tremendous applause to accept their awards: Lifelong Freedom of the City of Serannian, and election to the Roll of Heroes. The latter, without doubt, was the greatest honor Kuranes could confer. Limnar Dass was then promoted to Admiral of the King's Fleet, and

Gytherik—this time proceeding to the podium on his own account—became dreamland's first official Grand Master of Gaunts; and the names of both men were likewise entered on the Roll of Heroes. So the award-giving went on.

Now that the limelight was centered on persons outside the ken of Hero and company, they made their way out of the crush and to one side of the hall, where they could talk in something approaching privacy. "Something puzzles me," said Hero. "What of the poor brave lads who died during the battle? Are they destined to end up in Zura's Charnel Gardens?"

Limnar shook his head. "Oh, no, not them. They died willingly, bravely, not in horror. They were worthy warriors, dying as warriors have always died. No, Zura has no claim on them. Besides, Serannian burns her dead. There's little enough room on the sky-island for the living, let alone the dead."

"Huh!" grunted Eldin. "There's not so much damned room for David Hero and Eldin the Wanderer, either! I mean, what use is the freedom of the city to us? The longer we stay here, the sooner we'll come face to face with the Curator. We were damned lucky he didn't spot us today. And now that we know what he's capable of . . ."

"How come he's not here, anyway?" asked Gytherik. "I should have thought he was the greatest hero of us all?"

"Oh, but the Curator wasn't protecting Serannian," Limnar explained. "He was protecting the Museum. As for honoring him: would he come if we asked him? Doubtful. Would he even understand? No one can say. The Curator is . . . the Curator."

"Damn right he is," Eldin agreed, "and he's bloody dangerous!"

Done with the handing out of the more important awards and having passed on his duties to Serannian's mayor, Kuranes spied the group of four where they stood in quiet conversation. He immediately made his way through the crowd toward them. "So there you are," he said, smiling. "I wondered where you'd got to. Tonight I'm having a few friends round to may place. You're invited."

"Ah!" said Hero. "As your Majesty knows, we're not much at polite conversation, Eldin and I, and—"

"It's in your honor," Kuranes quickly shut him up, "and you'll come. All of you."

Gytherik shook his head. "Lord Kuranes, such as I'd like to, I can't come," and he went on to explain his mission. "So you see," he finished, "while Hero, Eldin and Limnar here are finished with their quest, mine is only just beginning. When my gaunts are fully rested, then I'll be off."

"We were thinking of going with him," added Eldin.

"Me, too," Limnar Dass hastily put in, "er—with your permission, of course."

"The egg of a shantak-bird, eh?" Kuranes scratched his ear thoughtfully. "Far Inquanok, you say? That's very interesting. It's also a shame—that you should have to go so far, I mean—when there's a shantak's egg much closer than that."

"There is!" Gytherik had to restrain himself from physically grabbing hold of the King. "But where?"

"Most people," said Kuranes, "when visiting the Museum, get no farther than the ground floor. Men being what they are, they would rather gaze upon treasures than the wonders and beauties of Nature."

"There's a shantak's egg in the Museum!" gasped Gytherik.

The King nodded. "On the top floor, where the windows face in the direction of Oriab. Twelve inches long and dark red in color, it's quite unmistakable . . ."

The four glanced at each other with eyes that were suddenly bright under raised, speculative eyebrows. Then, as the King began to speak again, they quickly assumed looks of bland innocence.

"But perhaps I shouldn't have mentioned it," Kuranes continued, "for of course there's no possible way you could get hold of it. Why, the greatest thieves in all the dreamlands couldn't do it!" He gave a wry chuckle, then quickly sobered. "As for tonight: very well, Gytherik, I shan't expect to see you. Neither you nor your friends, Hero and Eldin." He turned to an agitated Limnar Dass and smiled. "It would be a matter of serious ingratitude if we should allow benefactors such as these to proceed unaided, wouldn't you say, Limnar? Can you scrape a crew together before the fall of night?"

"Majesty," said the other, "with your permission . . . I've already done so!" And all of them, including Kuranes, burst into glad laughter.

The Curator stood in night-black shadows on the top floor of the dark and silent Museum and gazed west at the fabulous city of Serannian. Ineffably strange and monstrously metallic, he was motionless as some suit of alien armor.

He knew that there were human beings in the city with designs on certain of his possessions, knew also that they were on their way here even now. Out on the face of the Cerenerian, less than a mile away and light-less as a pirate, one of Kuranes' ships lay in wait; and this also the Curator knew. He knew many things, this anomaly in Earth's dreamland, including the difference between good and evil, between right and wrong. The difference between a shantak's bird's egg and a giant ruby . . .

Now, with the very faintest whir of miniature mechanisms, his head tilted to gaze skyward. Black as night that sky, and cloudy, but bright as day to the Curator. Four gaunts silently circling, and others keeping their distance. And the four were burdened with a pair of black-garbed human figures. A strange blue gleam came into the Curator's crystal eyes.

After a moment or two there came the very lightest of bumps upon the Museum's roof, as if a pair of doves had alighted there, but the Curator knew their purpose—knew even their weight, the temperature of their skins, the number of hairs standing excitedly erect upon their necks. And he waited silently in the shadows as they lowered themselves from the roof and in through a hole blown in the Museum's wall by one of Zura's cannon balls.

In another moment the pair were tip-toeing down the length of the Museum's upper hall, and now they paused at that massive open cabinet wherein a thousand eggs—from that of the tiniest hummingbird of jungled Kled to that of the great roc of Hnareth—were housed in all their diverse beauty. All except the egg of the shantak-bird!

Confounded, the adventurers turned to one another. Frowning, Eldin jerked his thumb toward the huge cabinet and raised his eyebrows in puzzled inquiry. Hero shrugged and cast about large-eyed and anxious in the darkness. And silently, unseen, the Curator glided forward, his crystal eyes glowing a metallic blue and firmly centered upon the pair who stood wrapped in indecision and black disappointment.

With a second shrug, Hero turned to the windows

where they looked toward the southeast. Eldin joined him and they vainly searched for a latch or some other form of fastening. While they were thus occupied, the Curator loomed gleamingly large out of the shadows behind them. And in the same instant, finally the two sensed his presence. Hair standing on end, they whirled, gazed into blue-glowing crystal eyes, reached suddenly spastic fingers toward swords—

—And froze as the blue glow bathed them in waves of light!

The Curator had no need of stealth now. He clanked around the pair and stepped up to the window, which slid easily to one side at his approach. The adventurers saw him clearly—saw every move he made—but were completely incapable of movement. Only their eyes were alive in bodies utterly bereft of will.

Now the Curator's gaze went out across the Cerenerian and found Limnar's ship where she rocked gently in darkness. The light in his eyes turned shimmering silver, shot out from his face and lit the ship in a blinding glory ...

High over the Museum where he rode his great gaunt in cool night air, Gytherik was dazzled by the light. For a moment he jerked his gaze away, then slitted his eyes to look again. Two tiny figures were moving rapidly, automatically along the silvery beam from Museum to ship, their speed slowing as, at the end of their ride, they were gently deposited upon the deck. Then the silver beam blinked out.

By the time the gaunt-master set his grim down on the deck of Limnar's ship, Hero and Eldin were just beginning to recover from their paralysis. Limnar and his crew, still astonished, surrounded the pair where they sat in an unbelieving daze. Then Gytherik saw the large, pear-shaped object which Hero held in his trembling hands and pounced upon it with a joyful whoop.

For of course it was the dark red egg of shantak-bird . . .

An Epilogue, of Sorts

Two men sat in bamboo chairs on the porphyry balcony of a rather exclusive tavern high over the harbor of Baharna. Below them, haphazardly terraced, the many flights and levels of the town went steeply down to the wharves, beyond which the night stars floated on the mirror surface of the harbor. Sweet scents of summer suppers, cooked outdoors in the warmth of early night, floated up to them where they sat lost in reverie.

Eldin's mind gentled thoughts of the girls he and Hero had found on their first night in the town, virgin twins well educated—and well past the marrying age—who had fallen in with the adventurers with a willingness previously outside the Wanderer's experience. It had been as if they deliberately sought defloration, and of course neither he nor Hero had anything special against that. For one idyllic week they had played escorts and lovers to these beauties, but always with the faint suspicion that there was something mercenary or at the very least dilettantish in the attitudes of those ladies. Even now the twins, Ula and Una, were taking scented baths in apartments paid for by the adventurers,

and soon that wily pair of worthies would put aside
their exotic drinks and go up to them.

As to why Hero and Eldin were here in Baharna on
the Isle of Oriab: well, why not? Hero had never visited
here before, and the Wanderer had always told the most
fabulous and outrageous tales of the place. Moreover,
this was that island where loomed those hollow mountains whose roots went down to the underworld.
Gytherik had been headed this way, and so they had
been willing to go along with him. Alas, his impatience
had precluded their own involvement in the rescue of
his father; for having spent little more than a day with
them aboard Limnar's ship, Gytherik had said his farewells, mounted his great gaunt and departed with his
grim—not to mention the shantak's egg—to do the job
on his own. Doubtless all had worked out as desired
and both Mathur and his gaunt-master son were now
back home in Nir. At least it suited Eldin's purpose to
think so.

As for Limnar Dass: having put the adventurers
ashore he, too, had taken his leave of them. He had his
own woman in Serannian, whom he intended shortly to
marry, and so would not allow himself to be tempted by
Baharna's fleshpots or the females who frequented
them. And since Gytherik had long since gone off on
his own . . . well, Limnar really had no excuse now for
the avoidance of his new duties. And so he had sailed
away from Oriab, and the last the adventurers had seen
of him was his ship of dreams, far out on the Southern
Sea, rising up from the water and cleaving for the
clouds.

As Eldin mulled over these not unpleasant, slightly
poignant thoughts, Hero was involved with rather
blacker visions. Namely, what he would like to do to a
certain thief if only he knew who he was and where to

find him. For only last night, in the absence of the adventurers and their lady friends, their rooms had been
entered and most of their money stolen. This had been
a not inconsiderable purse, a personal reward from
Kuranes, and its loss might well have proved embar-
rassing. Fortunately they had been able to pay their bills
with their golden medals of heroism, but to actually part
with those hard-won honors had not at all been to their
liking.

Still, they were all paid up for once, and they still
had a tond or two, their good new clothes, and the com-
panionship of the lovely girls upstairs. But for that
damned thief, they might easily have idled away another fortnight here. Hero pictured himself crushing the
windpipe of their unknown malefactor.

"Not if I got to him first," said Eldin.

Hero started. "Eh? Can you read minds then?"

"You were growling to yourself," the Wanderer
pointed out. "And you were curling your lip a bit."

Hero was forced to give back a wry grin. "It's just
that being a thief," he explained, "I hate being robbed!
And talking about robbery, it was your turn to get the
drinks two rounds ago."

Eldin nodded affably. "I thought you'd missed it," he
said. "Are you sure you want another? Ula and Una
will be wondering where we are."

"They'll not go off the boil," Hero answered. "Damn
me, I can't understand how two such ladies retained
their virginity for so long! Can you? I mean, they're
man-eaters. Why, I must have lost twenty pounds!"

"I know," Eldin grinned. "Wonderful, isn't it? I'll get
the drinks." He stood up and passed through bead curtains into the barroom, leaving Hero to return to his
dire, vengeful imaginings.

A minute or so later, just as Hero was settling back

into his less than restful reverie, Eldin returned clutching a folded handbill. He was in something of a hurry and his face displayed a slightly lighter color than its norm. Puzzled, Hero asked, "Where's my drink? And why the worried look?"

Making a visible effort to remain calm, Eldin sat; and in answer to Hero's questions he spread the poster on their table. It was a WANTED notice and told, more or less, the following tale:

That the twin daughters of the merchant Ham Gidduf of Andahad, a small but rich seaport on the far side of Oriab, had been abducted from their home only ten days before they were to be presented to the twin Dukes of Isharra, who would be visiting the island in their search for suitable brides. The girls had spent the last six years in a nunnery on the mainland until their father could find the right match for them. Ham Gidduf—obviously a rich man—was hereby placing a reward for ten thousand tonds on the head of the abductor, dead or alive, or seven thousand on each head should there prove to be more than one. He also offered a fat reward for any conclusive information. The handbill was to be given wide circulation.

"Where'd you get this?" Hero asked, his voice calm as his mind raced.

"From a big, hard-looking bully-boy," Eldin answered. "Half-a-dozen of them just came into the bar, all armed to the teeth. They look like freelance bounty hunters to me." As Hero stood up, the Wanderer parted the bead curtains a little and peeped out. "Oh, oh!" he warned. "One of them is talking to the proprietor—and another is chatting with the old boy who has the room next to ours."

"Did they see you duck out here?" Hero asked, his voice tight now.

"I don't think so," Eldin answered. "Why should they watch me? Do I look like ... like an abductor? No, don't answer that." Still peering out through the curtains, he stiffened.

"What is it?" Hero hissed.

"That's torn it!" Eldin answered. "The one who was talking to our next door neighbor is looking this way, and he's got a sly grin on his face. And ... yes, here he comes!"

"Get behind the plant," said Hero.

As Eldin ducked behind a huge potted palm, Hero quickly seated himself facing the curtains. He sprawled casually in his chair and toyed with an empty tankard. A moment later the curtains parted to admit a short, brutish-looking thug with the build of a rhino. Straight up to Hero he stepped, his hand resting lightly on the hilt of his sword. "David Hero?" he growled.

"Um?" said Hero laconically. "Did you say something?"

"I said, is your name Hero?" the other loudly repeated as Eldin slipped out from behind the palm and came up behind him.

"That's me," said Hero, making as if to stand. The thug began to slide his sword from its scabbard but had moved it less than an inch when Eldin delivered a rabbit punch that would have felled a roc. Hero caught him as he fell and lowered him quietly to the floor. He turned to Eldin.

"Right," he said, "let's go!" They stepped to the balustrade, swung their legs across and began to climb down toward the precarious roofs, spidery bridges and narrow, steeply-angled streets below.

"Oh, let's go by all means," said Eldin. "But go where?" Hero made no answer.

They climbed down onto a street narrow as a ledge

and paused for a moment in friendly shadows. Suddenly, somewhere up above, the night came alive with muffled cries of astonishment rapidly turning to outrage. Moments later there came loud and grateful sobs of relief in well known female voices, and finally hoarsely shouted orders and clattering sounds of hot pursuit.

"Now that the girls are no longer virgins," Hero whispered, "I don't suppose these Dukes of Isharra will be any too interested in them."

"That's right," Eldin agreed, "that's what it was all about. The girls were simply using us, and I think I know why. I've heard of this Isharra. Its people are backward types and all ugly as hell, particularly the so-called aristocracy. There's a goldmine there and the Dukes of Isharra—I'm not sure if they're real Dukes or if that's just their name—are the owners. The way I see it, Ula and Una have made damn sure they no longer qualify for the bridal procession! I imagine that when they were 'abducted,' they must have messed the place up and left Daddy a ransom note or some such. Now they'll be able to go home to Andahad again and find themselves a couple of likely lads to fall in love with. If old man Gidduf has bags of money, they'll manage that all right . . ."

"You're pretty shrewd for an old fool," said Hero. "Those girls made fools of both of us." He grinned mirthlessly.

"Maybe for the first day or so," Eldin nodded, "but after that . . . I think they would have liked to tell us."

"Except that would ruin the abducted bit, eh?" said Hero cynically. "Well, speaking for myself, I reckon a man's head is too high a price to pay for a mere maidenhead—especially when it was offered free of charge!"

"That's the difference between you and me," said Eldin. "I have romance in my soul . . ."

Hero snorted, then cocked his ear upward. Booted feet were running along the streets up there and someone was still shouting orders.

"A romantic, are you?" said Hero. "Well, maybe you are." He sighed. "I seem to remember that our recent adventures began with accusations of rape and other atrocities. If Ula and Una are telling the tale I think they're telling right now, we're about to be accused again!" He moved to the low wall, stepped over it, looked down once, and with the agility of a monkey began to descend.

Close behind him, Eldin grunted, "Aye, and this time you can include abduction—and the dreamlands are full of bounty hunters these days. *And* . . . you still haven't told me where we're going."

"Going?" Hero replied as he nimbly jumped free of the rough stone face. The moon turned him to a fleeting silhouette in the instant before he lightly landed upon a fairly flattish roof. "Why—we're going on, of course—we're going on!"

And together they fled into the night . . .

BRIAN LUMLEY

☐	51199-9	DEMOGORGON	$4.99
☐	50832-7	THE HOUSE OF DOORS	$4.95
☐	52137-4	NECROSCOPE	$5.99
☐	52126-9	VAMPHYRI! Necroscope II	$4.95
☐	52127-7	THE SOURCE Necroscope III	$4.95
☐	50833-5	DEADSPEAK Necroscope IV	$4.95 Canada $5.95
☐	50835-1	DEADSPAWN	$4.99 Canada $5.99
☐	52032-7	PSYCHAMOK	$5.99
☐	52023-8	PSYCHOMECH	$5.99
☐	52030-0	PSYCHOSPHERE	$5.99

Buy them at your local bookstore or use this handy coupon:
Clip and mail this page with your order.

Publishers Book and Audio Mailing Service
P.O. Box 120159, Staten Island, NY 10312-0004

Please send me the book(s) I have checked above. I am enclosing $ _____
(Please add $1.25 for the first book, and $.25 for each additional book to cover postage and handling.
Send check or money order only—no CODs.)

Name _____
Address _____
City _____ State/Zip _____
Please allow six weeks for delivery. Prices subject to change without notice.

SPINE-TINGLING
® HORROR FROM TOR

☐ 52061-0	**BLOOD BROTHERS** *Brian Lumley*	$5.99 Canada $6.99
☐ 51970-1	**BONEMAN** *Lisa Cantrell*	$4.99 Canada $5.99
☐ 51189-1	**BRING ON THE NIGHT** *Don & Jay Davis*	$4.99 Canada $5.99
☐ 51512-9	**CAFE PURGATORIUM** *Dana Anderson, Charles de Lint & Ray Garton*	$3.99 Canada $4.99
☐ 50552-2	**THE HOWLING MAN** *Charles Beaumont, edited by Roger Anker*	$4.99 Canada $5.99
☐ 51638-9	**THE INFLUENCE** *Ramsey Campbell*	$4.50 Canada $5.50
☐ 50591-3	**LIZZIE BORDEN** *Elizabeth Engstrom*	$4.99 Canada $5.99
☐ 50294-9	**THE PLACE** *T.M. Wright*	$4.95 Canada $5.95
☐ 50031-8	**PSYCHO** *Robert Bloch*	$3.95 Canada $4.95
☐ 50300-7	**SCARE TACTICS** *John Farris*	$4.95 Canada $5.95
☐ 51048-8	**SEASON OF PASSAGE** *Christopher Pike*	$4.50 Canada $5.50
☐ 51303-7	**SOMETHING STIRS** *Charles Grant*	$4.99 Canada $5.99

Buy them at your local bookstore or use this handy coupon:
Clip and mail this page with your order.

Publishers Book and Audio Mailing Service
P.O. Box 120159, Staten Island, NY 10312-0004

Please send me the book(s) I have checked above. I am enclosing $ _____
Please add $1.25 for the first book, and $.25 for each additional book to cover postage and handling.
Send check or money order only—no CODs.)

Name _____

Address _____

City _____ State/Zip _____

Please allow six weeks for delivery. Prices subject to change without notice.